THE
HUMILIATIONS
OF
WELTON
BLAKE

DISCARDED

ALEX WHEATLE

Barrington Stoke

For all those comic writers of The Beano, Whizzer and Chips, The Dandy *and* Shoot! *who kept this young boy's spirits up when it was most needed*

First published in 2021 in Great Britain by
Barrington Stoke Ltd
18 Walker Street, Edinburgh, EH3 7LP

www.barringtonstoke.co.uk

Text © 2021 Alex Wheatle

The moral right of Alex Wheatle to be identified as the
author of this work has been asserted in accordance with the
Copyright, Designs and Patents Act, 1988

A CIP catalogue record for this book is available
from the British Library upon request

ISBN: 978-1-78112-949-4

Printed by Hussar Books, Poland

CONTENTS

CHAPTER 1

The Worst Day in the History of Everything

It was one of those days when everything went madly wrong. One of those unlucky days when the forecast was for Tornado Bad Luck to come your way with hailstones the size of basketballs.

It all started in the morning. I woke up and found my mobile phone had died. It refused to charge. No matter what buttons I pressed, it wouldn't switch on. Not even a flicker. Not even a small white dot in the middle of the screen. I took out the SIM card and put it back fifteen times. Sweet diddly nothing.

I should've taken that as a sign that my day wasn't gonna be blessed. I should've faked a brain-ache and stayed in bed. But, oh no, I didn't do that. I swung my toes out of bed and planted them on the floor.

I dragged myself to the kitchen. Ever since I'd started secondary school, I had to make my own breakfast. I had my regular two slices of toast and a glass of mango juice. Then I grabbed a fistful of peanuts from a bag I'd bought the evening before. Mum was going on about her boyfriend visiting later on. I didn't give her twittering too much attention.

At the breakfast table I tried switching my phone on again and ... nothing. Not even a slight vibration. How was I going to text the great love of my life, Carmella McKenzie? Even worse, how was she gonna text me? It'd taken me four months to build up the courage to chat to her. I'm talking about the kind of bravery like Luke Skywalker stepping out in front of Kylo Ren's space fleet with just his lightsaber.

Carmella was one of the most delicious-looking females in the school. No, delete that. She was *the* A-plus, top-rated girl in the school. Skin the colour of caramel, deep brown chestnut eyes, cute gold stud in her nose and a smile wider than the Millennium Falcon.

After school yesterday, I don't know what got into me. There Carmella was at the bus stop. Alone. She had her headphones on. She was bobbing her head to her music. There weren't any of her friends in sight to boy-block me. It was a once-in-a-lifetime chance. I took a deep breath. *This is the moment*, I told myself.

I took in a lungful of air and stepped up to her, Jedi-style. I slowed down when I was about ten paces away. Now was the time to deliver my cool walk. I'd been practising it on the balcony of our block of flats. There was a kind of bounce and a dip to the walk. My body leaned to the right. I hadn't worked out exactly what to do with my arms, so I decided to swing them with my left shoulder higher than the other. The movement strained my neck and my side, but it was for a most important cause.

"Hi, Carmella," I said.

"Hi, Blakey," she replied. I normally didn't love being called Blakey, but Carmella could get away with it because she was super-pretty. "What's happening?"

I tried to look as cool as possible. I put on my best pose. It hurt my back, but it had to be done.

"You all right, Welton?" she asked. She looked proper worried, like a really sweet nurse caring for a cancer patient who only had three minutes to live. I couldn't believe she'd called me Welton.

"Do you ..." I started. "There ... There's this film. Yes, there's this film that's showing in the cinema. You know, the one in the Orchard shopping centre ... the cinema there. Films show there. In the afternoon and evenings."

"I know where the cinema is, Welton. I was born in these ends."

There was this tiny percentage of a smile starting at the corners of Carmella's mouth. Mr Mountjoy, my hairy Maths teacher, would call it about 2 per cent. At that moment I rated my chances of going to the movies with Carmella McKenzie at less than 0.011 per cent. By now, my back was really hurting from my pose.

"Can ... can I take you to see a film?"

My legs turned to pasta as I waited for Carmella's answer. I started to sweat like a Sumo wrestler in a sauna. My heart started to sprint like a Jamaican relay-runner.

"Yeah, all right," she said. "Call me to tell me what day, what time the film starts and where to link."

"I ... yes, of course I'll call you. Thanks so much ... I haven't got your number. I need your number to call you. You know. Otherwise I can't call you. This is soooo wicked! Thanks so much for saying yes."

She smiled. This time it was about 30 per cent. My heart stopped vibrating inside my throat. I wiped the sweat from my forehead. My palm couldn't have been wetter if I'd dipped it in a lake during a monsoon.

We swapped numbers. My brain was rushed with pictures. Sydney Harbour as the clock ticked to 12.01 a.m. on New Year's Day. The Olympics closing ceremony. The whole of Middle Earth bowing to four hobbits. Luke Skywalker, Han Solo and Chewbacca receiving their gongs from Princess Leia in *Episode IV*.

I had got over one of my worst fears and asked a girl out. But now, a day later, my phone had deleted itself. *How am I gonna link with Carmella and set a time for our date?* It was the worst crisis I had ever had in my life. Well, maybe not the worst. Dad leaving home for another woman might have topped it. I could still remember finding Mum in the early hours of the morning curled up in a corner of the kitchen. She'd been crying lakes. It'd taken me the length of a *Star Wars* boxset to persuade Mum to go to her bed.

But I couldn't log on to my parents' issues right now. I had to use my Jedi powers to clear away Carmella's boy-blocking friends, step up to her and tell her my plans for our date.

CHAPTER 2

School

As I headed out, Mum said that I should get home on time so that I didn't miss the breaking news she had to tell me. I wasn't really listening. After every twenty words that Mum said, I replied all right or OK. In between those words I nodded. If I kept to that, she wouldn't pull me around to face her and ask, *Are you listening to me, Welton?* It was one of those dumb questions that parents asked. I mean, I was never going to say no.

I reached school, Monks Orchard High, about five minutes before lessons started. I searched for Carmella. Couldn't find her. The peanuts I had eaten earlier were causing my insides some grief, but there was no time to think about that before my first lesson – Maths.

My Maths teacher, Mr Mountjoy, was simply the hairiest man in the history of the galaxy. He was like a walking jungle. One time he stopped to look at my work and pressed his hand on my exercise book. I swear there were fungi, toadstools, Amazonian bushes, apple orchards and banana leaves growing out of his skin. And the stench coming from his armpits wasn't exactly fresh. His nose hair was gross. I wouldn't be kidding if I said that Tarzan and his pet chimp could have swung on those things.

I took a desk by the window that overlooked the playground. I glanced through the glass every now and again to see if Carmella might be arriving late. What would happen if she was sick and out of action for the coming week? Would our date still be on?

Maybe she'd got ill on purpose? Maybe she'd had second thoughts. That must be it. After she'd said yes, she must've gone home and had a long think about the situation. *I said yes to go to the movies with Welton Blake? Are you sick, Carmella?* she would've asked herself. And now she couldn't come to school because the thought of it made her ill.

I was trying to work out what b and d were, and wondering what's the point of algebra, when I glanced out of the window again and spotted Carmella. She had this casual stride. Her hair was in a ponytail. Her caramel skin was glowing with pure niceness in the morning sun. She seemed to be happy about something.

Without realising it, I was smiling. Man! She was the main reason why school was bearable. If everything went to plan, I could soon be sitting next to Carmella with my arm around her watching a movie.

But wait! Carmella was walking across the playground with someone. She was with another bruv. I had never seen him before. He looked ripped enough to join the cast of *Fast & Furious*. I hated him instantly. I felt my heartbeat in my throat. The inside of my head was bubbling like my mum's casserole. Carmella and Muscle Freak stopped. She hugged him and kissed him on the cheek. I wanted to scream like Darth Vader at the end of *Revenge of the Sith*. Something was starting to move about in my chest. I hoped I wasn't about to give birth like that poor guy in the first *Alien* film.

"Welton Blake!" Mr Mountjoy yelled at me. "Is your exercise book stuck to the window?"

"No, sir," I replied.

"Then turn around and pay attention to the book on your desk!"

He started walking towards me.

Oh no.

Mr Mountjoy knelt down so his head was the same height as mine. He was wearing a white shirt and a yellow tie. His dandruff was as thick as the falling snow in Christmas movies. My stomach wanted my legs to run away.

"Do you understand what I have been telling you?" Mountjoy asked.

"Yes, sir," I said.

"Then get on with it!"

He walked away. Thank the Jedi stars for that.

But suddenly I felt sick. Something horrible was moving around in my throat. Mashed peanuts. Up and down it went. Down and up. Up and down. The combination of seeing Carmella hugging and kissing another guy together with Mountjoy's stench proved too much. Something surged within me.

Past experience told me that when you felt sick you made sure that you didn't get any of it over you when it came. So I stood up, leaned forward and puked over the girl sitting in front of me. Karen Francis. She had this lovely long ginger hair ... or she *did* have lovely long ginger hair. Her blouse and blazer were always spotless ... until now.

Karen got up from her chair all stiff, like a zombie in a bad horror film. Her blazer, collar and lovely mane of ginger hair were decorated with partly digested peanuts, bits of toast and last night's dinner – cheese and bacon flan, cabbage and potato salad. Her face slowly changed from one of disbelief into one of rage, Terminator-style. I wasn't sure why I didn't run like a rebel spacecraft being chased by Darth Vader's imperial fleet.

"WELTON BLAKE!" Karen screamed.

She launched herself at me, punching and kicking me until I fell off my chair. Mr Mountjoy didn't save me until after Karen had taken off her blazer and rubbed my face in it.

I got to my feet groggily. Bits of my own sick were on my tongue, in my nostrils and all over my face. It was the most dreadful thing I had ever tasted – even worse than the soggy cardboard I'd eaten for a dare the year before. Laughter was all around me. Karen Francis stormed out of the classroom swearing some words I'd never heard of.

"Get yourself cleaned up!" Mr Mountjoy shouted at me.

Roars of laughter filled my ears. These weren't chuckles or giggles. This was the kind of laughing that made people cry, lose control of their legs and wet themselves.

CHAPTER 3

The Boys' Toilets

I walked out of the classroom, my feet slapping the floor. It was just my luck that there weren't any toilets on this floor. I had to fly downstairs. I leapt down four steps at a time. Landing on the ground floor, I twisted my ankle. "Arrrggghhhh!"

I collapsed to the ground, took off my shoe and rubbed my ankle. Pure agonies went all the way up my right leg. I sensed a presence. I looked up and standing over me was the second most beautiful girl in my school – Alice Stanbury. She had long black hair, cute dimples and nice big eyes like a Japanese cartoon. I think her mum was Chinese and her dad was half Jamaican or something. Her skin shade was somewhere between milky coffee and that toffee sweet in the Quality Street tin. At this moment I felt the bits of sick on my cheeks, lips and forehead. I touched my chin and noticed I was bleeding.

"Oh, er ... hi, Alice."

Alice said nothing. She looked at me as if I had fallen into a really deep volcano that was erupting with gorilla crap. Her face sort of scrunched up before she half-screamed, "Eeeewwwww!"

I got up and limped the rest of the way to the boys' toilets. I didn't look back, but I guessed Alice Stanbury was watching me with 99.9 per cent disgust.

I put my right ankle under the cold tap and waited for five minutes, hoping the water would numb my pain. The floor was damp with urine, as it always was. A toxic stench polluted the air from the last cubicle. I looked into the mirror and asked myself, "How did it all go sooooo wrong?" And, "Why, why, why did I get out of bed this morning?"

Who was this guy with Carmella? Why didn't she tell me she had a boyfriend? How many times has he kissed Carmella? I wished for his crusty body to be pulped into a bloody nothingness by Optimus Prime or some other Transformer. I imagined Carmella and Mr Muscles getting married on on some live TV dating show.

I cleaned myself up with paper towels and decided to take a low profile for the rest of the school day. My breath still stank of sick and I had vomit stains all over my blazer and shirt. My ankle throbbed and I had this worm-shaped cut on my chin. There was no way I could face Carmella.

I remained in the boys' toilets during break time. I tried to put weight on my ankle. "Arrrggghhhh!"

My common sense told me to go and see the nurse so she could send me home. But because I was hurt, I knew she wouldn't let me go home on my own. She would have to inform Mum. No way was Mum coming to the school to pick me up! Even if the mighty Chewbacca ate my ankle with salt and pepper on top, I still wouldn't ask for Mum to collect me. I just couldn't risk Carmella seeing me being helped by my mum out of the school. That would be a humiliation too far.

CHAPTER 4

50p for an Insult

At lunchtime I hobbled to the school library. None of the cool people went there, only the friendless, the book folk, the really bored and the five-star students who did their homework on time. I just wanted to be left alone.

"Blakey!"

Man! I hated my nickname. I looked up. It was Nicholas Fumbold. A kid in my year who always hung around with the cool kids but wasn't cool himself.

What did he want? Nicholas liked to argue. We had a row for over a week when he claimed *The Phantom Menace* was better than *The Empire Strikes Back*. Was he insane? My mum told me there were blasphemous things in the bible, but nothing in there could compare to what Fumbold said. I told him he should beat himself with a really hot lightsaber a million and one times.

"What you doing up here?" he asked. "Been looking for you all dinner time ... What's that smell?"

"What do you want, Fumbold?"

"I want to buy an insult."

I haven't mentioned yet that I made a few pennies by selling cusses and insults at school. I was picked on during the first year of secondary and I discovered that if I was funny, the bad boys would sometimes leave me alone.

It dawned on me now that if there was still a very slight chance that I would be taking Carmella McKenzie out to the movies, I needed funds. Since Dad had left home my budget wasn't as pretty as it used to be. And I couldn't let Carmella buy her own popcorn or hot dogs. Noooo way! I reckoned she was the kind of girl who liked Minstrels or Maltesers. Not sure why.

"What kind of insult do you want?" I asked Fumbold.

"A mother one," Fumbold replied. "This girl in a lower year said something about my mum and everyone cracked up."

"Fifty pence," I demanded.

"Fifty pence? It was thirty pence last week."

"Do you wanna be cussed out by a girl in a younger year or do you want lyrics to fire back?" I asked.

Fumbold thought about it. His humiliation must've been tragic otherwise he wouldn't have been looking for me.

"All right," he said. His right hand searched for the jingles in his trouser pocket. "This better be top ranking!"

I took the cash from him and placed it in my own trouser pocket. "All right," I said, "tell her this: her mum is so ugly that when she was born, the doctor made a mistake and slapped the afterbirth."

"What?" Fumbold asked, looking as if I'd just spoken about A-level Physics. "What's an afterbirth?"

"It's the ..." I began, then shook my head. What a mud-brain! It was no surprise he thought *The Phantom Menace* was better than *The Empire Strikes Back*. No wonder this girl could cuss him out.

"When a baby is born, the baby comes out, right?" I explained. "And also, this other bit comes out. It's all gooey, sticky, slimy and fleshy, like the inside of a big uncooked chicken. Haven't you ever seen your mum clean a chicken?"

"No," Fumbold said.

"Anyway, that bit is called the afterbirth."

"Gross!" responded Fumbold. "But it's proper inspired!"

"Right, it's gross," I said. "So this girl's mum is so ugly, the doctor thought the afterbirth was the baby. Get it?"

Fumbold's face curved into an evil smile. He liked his purchase. A satisfied customer.

CHAPTER 5

Metalwork

After lunch, I had Metalwork. We were making these metal peg things, but I couldn't focus on my task because Harry Stanley, the class clown, was imitating my vomiting of earlier. It seemed the whole school had heard about me emptying my insides into the lovely ginger hair of Karen Francis.

I tried to ignore it, but a few of Harry's friends joined in. They all made this retching and spewing sound. Mr Prang, my Metalwork teacher, was in his little office on the phone. He always told us what we had to make, then only ever came out of his office if a kid sawed off his thumb, drilled into someone's ear or went nuts with a nail-gun. So, unless I drew blood myself, I would have to put up with Harry's fake projectile vomiting for the whole lesson.

But there was only so much I could take, especially after the morning I'd had, so when Harry kept going on, I roared, "JUST FREAKING LEAVE ME ALONE!"

At the precise moment I half-swore, Mr Prang came out of his office. Everyone stood still.

"Mr Blake," he said to me in a near whisper. He called everyone Mister – even girls, eleven year olds and sausage dogs. "You are aware that I detest profanity in my workshop, aren't you, Mr Blake?"

At least he never called me Blakey.

"Yes, sir, but it wasn't a full swear word," I said.

"Half an hour detention this afternoon."

Detention! My day can't get any worse even if bullies force me to watch re-runs of The Phantom Menace.

CHAPTER 6

Detention

After the last lesson of the day, I made my way to Mrs Swanson's room, where I would serve my detention. In a strange way, being in detention was perfect. No one would see me on the way home, especially Carmella. I had suffered tragedy, despair and shame today, but I was still breathing. My ankle bone might've been crushed into powder, but things were looking up for me.

Tomorrow, I'd wear clean garms. My breath would be passable. My ankle would finally stop throbbing and I'd be ready to face Carmella. Hopefully every student in the school would've forgotten about my projectile vomiting – and my beatdown from Karen Francis. And in a few days' time, I'd be going to the movies with Carmella. All that pain and humiliation would be worth it.

Mrs Swanson was the school's drama teacher and, like most drama teachers, she was, well, slightly bonkers ... Actually, no, not slightly but proper bonkers and a bit over-dramatic. Today, she was sitting on her desk wearing an African long shirt thing and this green and white scarf around her head.

"Welton! Welton!" Mrs Swanson welcomed me like a long-lost relative. "What cruel twist of fate brings you here? Take a seat, Welton. You will be reading *An Inspector Calls*."

I recognised some of the other students serving detention with me. Timothy Smotheram, known for his stink bombs and being a champion farter. Coral Chipglider, the school's spit and bogey queen. And ... *Oh no! Yoda be merciful!* Bernice Cummings! Bernice was one of Carmella's mates and I hated her almost as much as school Brussel sprouts. She had muscles in her ear lobes, biceps bigger than hovercraft bumpers and she walked like an angry cowboy. There was no doubt that she would tell Carmella I had turned up in detention smelling less than fresh.

I settled at a desk in a corner as far away as possible from Coral and Bernice. It was next to Timothy Smotheram, but I reasoned that it was better for my health to suffer one of his fatal farts than be drowned in Coral's spits or beaten by Bernice's right hook.

I noticed Coral staring at me like a poor kid in a poor country might gaze at a cream cake. She didn't blink once. *What's with her?* I thought. Man! She was proper intimidating.

Then Bernice turned around and looked at me as if I had crapped on her pillow. I couldn't work out what I had done to upset her. I tried to focus on reading *An Inspector Calls*, but every time I glanced up, Bernice glared at me with evil Sith-like eyes.

With a flourish of her arms, Mrs Swanson told us, "I have to get something from the staffroom. I'll be back before you can say house lights and stage right." She windmilled her arms again, then was gone.

As soon as she disappeared, Bernice Cummings stood up from her chair. She walked towards me and I remembered that scene in *Jurassic Park* when the Tyrannosaurus Rex planted a big heavy foot in the mud. I should've hyper-toed out of there, but I knew I wouldn't get far with my ankle.

Bernice pulled me up by the lapels of my school blazer. My feet barely touched the ground. She caught the scent of something nasty. My breath was still full of toxic sick fumes.

"What ... what is it, Bernice?" I managed.

"Did you sell an insult to Fumbold?" she wanted to know. Tiny bits of cheesy puffs flew into my face. They stuck on my cheeks.

My mind had a big fat question mark in it. Surely Fumbold wouldn't be so dumb as to say to right-hook happy *Bernice* that her mother was so ugly that when she was born the doctor slapped the afterbirth. Surely not.

Bernice pulled my face towards hers. I smelled the cheese real strong. There were bits of a chocolate caramel bar between her teeth. I was losing the feeling in my legs when she slammed me against the wall. "Fumbold insulted my little sister!" she raged. She slapped me across the forehead with her Chewbacca-like paw. I could feel the vibrations in my toes.

"I didn't know the insult was for her," I squealed.

At times of intense panic or when I think I'm going to die, my voice goes into a high-pitched squeal for some reason. I was sure the local wolves and hounds could hear me.

I felt another crushing blow on my left cheek.

"She was very upset," Bernice added. She shoved my broken body into the wall again, her hands like mechanical grave diggers.

My voice went even higher. "I'm really sorry, Bernice. Really sorry."

She punched me in the stomach and I dropped to the floor. Satisfied, Bernice finally returned to her seat and casually picked up her copy of *An Inspector Calls*.

There were giggles as I staggered to my feet. As I went back to my chair, I was thinking that it must be some sort of record at the school for a boy to be beaten up by two girls in the same day.

Mrs Swanson returned and I read for a further ten minutes before we were given permission to leave. I allowed plenty of time for Bernice to disappear before I rose from my chair. As Coral left, she glared at me as if I'd spat on her granny.

CHAPTER 7

The Football Game

Timothy was hanging around waiting for me in the hallway outside the classroom door. "Are you still selling cusses?" he asked me.

Didn't he see me get a smackdown from Bernice? Was he insane? I rolled my eyes and walked past him. My body hurt all over and my ankle still felt like it'd been attacked by a peckish pack of hyenas. But I tried to walk normally. I didn't want to show anyone that I was a hospital case.

"Hold up," Timothy said. "It's not for Bernice's sister or anybody in this school. Between you and me, Bernice's sister is an evil little goblin. And if you spread that around, I'll deny it for ever and ever."

I stopped walking. Fifty pence is fifty pence. And if I could earn it without getting my blood cells boshed to different parts of my body, then so much the better. Maybe the jingles wouldn't go towards a cinema link with Carmella McKenzie, but I could buy a couple of chocolate bars on the way home. That would make me feel better at the end of my day from hell.

"OK," I agreed. "What kind of cuss do you want?"

"About being poor," Timothy said. His eyes got bigger and he opened his mouth. It was full of saliva. He moved closer and I got a strong whiff of his egginess. It was like someone lined his clothes with stale boiled eggs. It was overpowering and made my stomach do a little dance. I stood at an angle to Timothy so if I puked up it wouldn't be in his face or all over his brown hair.

"You had a 'being poor' argument," I said.

"Yeah," he said, nodding. "This rude girl who lives three doors away from me said my family's so poor that families living in a really poor country with a drought had sent food and water to us."

I swear that was an insult I sold a few months ago. I couldn't help but laugh a bit. Well, not a bit, I laughed a lot. In fact my stomach crunched up and I nearly fell to the floor. I could see in Timothy's eyes how much that insult had upset him. The pain in his expression told me that I had done my work well.

"Fifty p," I demanded.

Timothy handed me the cash. Man! "OK," I said, pocketing the money. "Tell her this. Say that her family is soooo poor that when her mum wanted wooden flooring she had to go to the park with a kitchen knife and strip the bark off an oak tree. Tell her that."

Timothy's grin started from the corners of his mouth and reached his eyes. As he opened his mouth, I got an extra blast of egginess, but it was worth it. Another satisfied customer.

"Excellent!" Timothy said, rubbing his hands like some evil scientist in an old horror film. "Excellent!"

I started walking away, but he called me back. "You're not gonna watch the football?"

"Football?" I repeated. "What football?"

"Our year is playing Miller's Pond High. Didn't you know?"

"No, I didn't."

Miller's Pond High were our main sporting rivals. This year they had beaten us at everything. Netball, hockey, and track and field. In football they'd murdered us 11 goals to 1 at their place. A few weeks ago in basketball they'd destroyed us 66 points to 12. During that defeat I thought our PE teacher, Mr Purrfoot, was gonna explode like the first Death Star.

"What's the point?" I finally replied to Timothy. "We're gonna lose big-time."

"Yeah," said Timothy. "And I'm gonna wind up every player on our team."

I liked the idea of that. It would make a nice change to watch someone else getting humiliated.

Timothy and I made our way to the back of the school and onto the sports grounds. We made a right pair: me with my vomit breath and him with his stale-egg stink.

The game had already started. I was about a hundred metres away, walking across the cricket square, when I saw him. Muscle Freak. The

Sith Lord who had hugged my Carmella. He was playing football for our school team. I couldn't believe it. I could see the muscles in his legs from where I stood. This demon was the reason for all my humiliation, pain and shame. Man, I wanted him to suffer.

I stopped in my tracks. Timothy, and the egginess that surrounded him, walked on. "Aren't you coming?" he asked.

"No, I'm gonna watch it from here," I said.

There was a decent crowd on the touchlines. I could see Bernice Cummings and ... Carmella.

Oh, for the life of Yoda, no!

I stepped back a few paces so she wouldn't catch sight of me. I wanted her new boyfriend to break his leg into a million and one pieces. I hoped a Miller's Pond High defender would tackle him mouth-high so he could never taste lips with a chick again.

Unfortunately, Carmella's boyfriend was pretty good. In fact, he was totally depressingly brilliant. I watched him dribble past defender after defender and hop past the goalkeeper, then casually tap the ball into an empty net. Our home support went cadazy. Carmella was jumping up and down, clapping her hands. She hadn't been that excited when I'd asked her out for a movie date.

I kneeled on the ground and punched the turf with my right fist, pure rage and bitterness overwhelming me. *Ouch!* It didn't make me feel any better. My total humiliation was now complete.

I was just thinking of running to the hills high above Monks Orchard to let out a mighty scream when I heard my name.

"WELTON! WELTON!"

Oh, sweet Yoda! That was Carmella's voice. She had seen me.

"WELTON! *WELTON!*"

I looked up. Carmella was waving her arms, trying to get my attention.

I felt this heat of shame and embarrassment burn within my body. I had no option. I had to sonic-boom out of there as fast as I could. It was obvious that she wanted to deliver the bad news in person. She didn't want to go to the movies no more, but she wanted to be polite about it. *Welton, I'm sooo sorry! I really like you and wanted to go to the movies with you, but I met someone else. It was love at first sight. You understand, don't you?*

Then she'd mention the dreaded f word. *There is no reason why we can't be friends. In fact, we can all be friends. We could still talk and hang out. Maybe we could do history homework together sometime?*

I didn't wanna be friends. I definitely didn't want to hang out. She could hyper-speed her history homework into a black hole at the far side of the galaxy.

Despite the state of my ankle, I turned on my heels and half ran, half hobbled out of the sports grounds. I fell over a couple of times, but I didn't care. Every third stride I looked behind me, checking to see if Carmella was following. She wasn't.

Panting heavily, I reached the bus stop five minutes later. I prayed for a bus to come soon. There was mud on my forehead, but I just couldn't be bothered to wipe it off. When the bus arrived, I took a seat upstairs at the back and told myself that at least my day couldn't get any worse.

CHAPTER 8

The Big Announcement

When I got home, I took off my blazer, threw it over my bedside chair and crashed on my unmade bed. I closed my eyes and began to go over all the crazy events of the day. One thought came to my mind. *Why am I soooo unlucky?*

A year or so ago, I was happily living in Ashburton. Back then, Dad and Mum weren't threatening to delete each other on the way back from the supermarket like they did when we arrived in Monks Orchard. I had a bus-load of friends, got invited to lots of birthday parties and I had many cousins to fling snowballs at. But my parents decided the only way they could afford to buy a house was if they moved out of Ashburton. So we ended up in Monks Orchard, the most uncool part of the galaxy.

On my first day at school here, everyone thought I was the bomb, with me coming from Ashburton. But then they realised I couldn't maul with the best of them and I wasn't a boy-soldier of an Ashburton drug gang, and the guys laughed out their ribs at me. The girls ignored me. Soon after, Brian Broxslater started to tax me.

Broxslater was my year's school bully. He originally came from the grimy ends of North Crongton. Everybody feared him. He wasn't that tall, just kind of thick and stumpy. He had legs like castle turrets, arms like giant German sausages and he had a moustache at twelve years old. Well, it wasn't a full grown-up moustache. But you could see the hair follicles, outline and shadow.

Because of his whiskers everyone agreed that Broxslater was the baddest fighter in our year – especially as he was a Crongtonian. None of us had ever seen him fight, but the whole first year he went unchallenged. I mean, what idiot would try to fight somebody who already had a moustache? He stood on patrol at the school gates before registration and stepped up to kids like me and whispered, "Tax for the Chancellor."

One look at his moustache and his huge fist and I would give him my jingles.

At least I hadn't bumped into Broxslater's taxing paws today. I had to be grateful for that now I was crashed on my bed.

I was hungry – not surprising after emptying most of my bodily contents into Karen Francis's hair. I hoped Mum had something in the fridge that I could heat up in the microwave. I got up and had a look. There was macaroni cheese on a plate from three days ago. If I didn't eat it a day after cooking, then why would I do so three days later?

I checked the cupboards. There weren't any cheese and onion or barbecue flavour crisps there, only salt and vinegar. There were no custard creams either – I think I finished them off a couple of days ago. I had to settle for four slices of toast and two mince pies I found at the back of the cupboard. The sell-by date was long gone, but I didn't care.

I poured a drink of flat Coke and settled on the sofa, my mashed-up ankle resting on a cushion, to watch my favourite film – *The Empire Strikes Back*.

I was monster-munching into my second slice of toast while the 20th Century Fox fanfare announced my film was about to start when I heard Mum coming in the front door.

"Are you home, Welton?" Mum called. "Welton?!"

"I'm in the front room, Mum."

Maybe she's got pizza?

Pausing my film, I heard two other voices. *Oh, Yoda, give me the Force, no!* Mum's boyfriend, Kingsley (who I'd branded Greyback because of his grey ponytail) and his five-year-old demon son, Devon. The Brat came running into the front room and jumped on my bad ankle. "Welton!" he yelled, while throwing his arms around my neck.

"Arrrrggghhhh!" I yelped. "Get off me! Get off me!"

If I'd had the strength to launch him into orbit, I would've done so. It wasn't something a Jedi Knight should say, cos they're meant to be good with kids, but, sweet Yoda, I didn't like Devon too much.

Mum entered the lounge. She had a big smile on her face. Greyback had his right arm around her. He was grinning like he had won a Naboo Starship or something. I couldn't see what Mum saw in him. I mean, Greyback was ancient. His hair was greying, obviously. He had ridges in his forehead, like you see in those wrinkly beef-flavoured crisps. He had hair in his ears and shaving bumps like mountains on his neck.

I couldn't work out why Mum wasn't worried that Greyback might be out on a date with her one night and just collapse and die of old age. I also couldn't work out how Greyback had managed to produce a kid at his age. I'd given this a lot of thought and decided that Greyback wasn't Devon's real dad. He couldn't be. Devon must be the satanic child of some prince of hell and Bernice Cummings's ugly aunt.

Mum had told me that Greyback was much more mature than my dad. But what was the point of dating someone much more responsible if death was whispering to him?

"How was your day, Welton?" Greyback asked me.

I'd had the worst day of anyone who had ever lived, but I wasn't about to tell Greyback all about it. "Not too bad," I replied.

"We've made a decision," Mum cut in, unable to stop grinning. It was like her smile had a lifetime battery wired to it.

What decision could this be? I wondered. Maybe they'd decided to send Devon to some far-off boarding school on the other side of the universe?

"Kingsley and Devon are moving in with us for a while," Mum blurted out.

I didn't quite register what Mum said. I sort of stared into space and lost all the feeling in my face. The throbbing in my ankle suddenly stopped and I had this out-of-body experience like I was looking down at myself from the ceiling. I was beginning to think I had died. I tried to sit up, but my body wouldn't move. I couldn't move my tongue or my mouth.

"Kingsley's struggling to pay the rent at his place, so I suggested he move in here with us until we can get somewhere bigger together. Makes sense, don't you think, Welton ... Welton?"

I think I passed out for a couple of seconds. Maybe a minute. This couldn't be. Greyback and the Brat that even hell would reject were going to live with us! What had I ever done to deserve this 18+ rated horror?

"Er, what?" I said, finally getting my mouth moving. "How? What was that? Moving in? Our place is too small ... Is Devon going to sleep on the couch?"

"Don't be silly, Welton," Mum said. "I have already ordered another single bed. Devon will be sleeping in your room. There's plenty of space in there. He'll be the younger brother you never had. I've seen how well you guys get along."

Aaaaaarrrrrgggghhhh!

Devon bounced up and down on my bad ankle and I let out a real scream. "Arrrrgggghhhh!"

"He's a lively one, isn't he?" Greyback laughed, ignoring my pain. "So full of energy all the time. I can hardly keep up with him."

Because you're too old, I thought.

Mum nodded. "Yes, he is lively," she said. "Just like Welton was at his age. It'll be great all of us living together. It'll give us a chance to save and get a bigger place. Who knows? Maybe we can go on holiday together? Jamaica?"

I imagined sitting on a plane next to the Brat for ten hours.

Aaaaarrrrgggghhhh!

Devon had to go.

"We've ordered pizza for this evening," Mum announced. "And we're going to sit down like a proper family to eat it."

Greyback kissed her on the cheek. The Brat bounced on my bad ankle yet again. I leaned in close to him. "If you jump on my leg once more," I hissed, "I'm gonna wait till you're sleeping, take you up to the church spire and drop you onto the concrete head-first. Do you know what will happen to your head after that? It will crack open and the inside of it will look like the pizza you're gonna eat but with added tomato sauce."

The Brat looked at me as if he was expecting me to laugh. I had my serious face on, like Luke Skywalker before he fought Darth Vader in *The Empire Strikes Back*.

"Dad, Dad," the Brat wailed. "Welton said he's gonna drop me off the church to land on my head!"

"He knows I was joking," I chuckled. I laughed so Mum and Greyback were really convinced I was messing around. I ruffled the Brat's hair and he sort of smiled, maybe 25 per cent, not sure whether to trust me.

*

Half an hour later we sat down around our small table in the kitchen and had pizza. I made sure I got my fair share of garlic bread. I couldn't help but worry about what Dad would make of Greyback and the Brat moving in. He didn't even know that Mum had a boyfriend. He always asked me if Mum was seeing someone else and I would answer no.

Living in his damp flat alongside every species of spider, cockroach and fly had slowly turned Dad insane. Well, not totally insane, but on some Saturday mornings he didn't bother to wash, shave, get out of his pyjamas or move from the couch. Even worse, I couldn't get the TV remote control out of his hands. I didn't want to add to Dad's depression by telling him Mum had a new boyfriend who seemed much more mature than him.

After the pizza, I took off to hide in my room. Mum followed me in and asked, "Aren't you happy that Kingsley and I are trying to make a life together?"

I wanted to say no, but if I did Mum would want to talk the rest of the night and try to convince me to connect with Greyback and spend some quality time with him. I couldn't see how we would have anything in common as he was so ancient. He worked as a security guard in the Orchard shopping centre and liked to wear his uniform everywhere he went. So embarrassing!

"Yeah, I'm happy, Mum ... How long do you think we'll be staying here before we move to a bigger place?"

"Maybe six to nine months."

I took a deep breath. *Six to nine months of the Brat sharing my room. Six to nine months! There's no way in the Star Wars universe that I'll last even six to nine nights without committing a murder most stinkful.*

Maybe I can live with Dad? Then again, no. I'm sick and tired of chasing all brands of spiders out of his bathtub, not getting my choice on his TV, and the fish and chip shop is a twenty-minute trek from his place. I'll have to run away. I'll live in the woods for six to nine months and live on squirrels or something. I'll use the Force to hunt food.

"Is there anything you want to say, Welton?" Mum said, using her gentle voice. "I know all this is a bit sudden and I'm sorry to spring it on you. We've been talking about it for ages, but we finally made a decision last night. We wanted to tell you together."

I didn't know what to say. Well, something came to my mind, but it would've been rude to say it. Something like, "Greyback's only got about fifteen years max in him, Mum. And that's if he's lucky. Dad might be immature, but at least he'll live longer, is a painter and decorator, and he'll decorate the hallway when you want it done." Instead, I suddenly thought that maybe I could use this moment to ask for something.

"Can ... can I have a new phone, Mum? Please!"

Mum put her hands on her hips and gave me the look that told me I had said something real dumb again. "My priority is to get the new bed and to make sure we have everything ready for when Kingsley and Devon move in," she said. "I'm afraid a new phone can wait."

"But, Mum, my phone doesn't work! It won't even switch on! It's dead."

"I'm sure you'll survive without a phone until your birthday."

"My birthday's three months away," I complained. "Mum, please! You can't do this to me. This is child abuse! It's having an effect on my mental health. You might as well throw me in Jabba the Hutt's dungeon."

"Stop being so dramatic, Welton," Mum said. "Having a new phone is not an emergency or even on the first page of my priorities! I could do with an upgrade myself, but I have to wait."

How could I make her see it was an emergency? I had to admit to myself there was now only a very slim chance that I would be taking Carmella McKenzie to the movies, but I still wanted to call her. Maybe I still had a 1 per cent chance of going to the movies with her. Then again, maybe not. It would be easier to get Carmella's official *"Sorry, Welton, I found somebody else"* talk on the phone rather than hearing it face to face.

God! Face to face! I didn't think I could handle that. It might push me over the edge. I might spontaneously combust. Or do something really stupid like cry in front of her. I was gonna end up like Dad: not bothering to wash or change my clothes, farting on the sofa and not going out on a Saturday.

"There are bills to pay," Mum said, and then she went off on one. When she went off on one, she always started with "there are bills to pay". "New school shirts, trousers and shoes to buy, but, oh no! Welton wants a new phone! Let's drop everything until Welton gets his new phone!"

"I get it, Mum," I said.

She gave me an evil look and stomped out of my room, my faint hope of a new phone going with her.

To be honest I wouldn't have minded going without shirts, trousers and shoes if it meant I got a new phone. Mum was too old to realise that kids of my age were judged by what type of phone you had. I could turn up at school wearing old tennis racquets on my feet, a baseball hat made out of cardboard and Oliver Twist's hand-me-downs, but if I had a cool phone, I'd be on point.

*

For the rest of the evening I tried to work out what I was going to do if I bumped into Carmella. Somehow, I had to regain my cool. The popular kids in my year owned the latest mobile phones, were good at sports, wore name-brand trainers and didn't get taxed by Broxslater. My ancient phone was a brick that didn't work, my trainers had no name and Broxslater still taxed me. So that left sport.

I was rubbish at football, even worse at cricket, so it would have to be basketball. I'd never really tried my best at basketball, but it seemed pretty simple. You just had to chuck a ball in a basket. *That's it*, I thought, *I will try out for our year's basketball team.* I decided I would go and see Mr Purrfoot the very next day.

CHAPTER 9

The Rhino with the Stinkin' Armpit

My dreams that night were filled with nightmares where I shared a bedroom with the Brat for over twenty years and he grew so big he could tax me and smack me down. I woke up early and tired, but I still felt determined to give this B-ball thing a real go. The swelling had gone down in my ankle and it felt a lot better. I used my deodorant stick to try to delete the vomit smell from my school jacket. I packed my PE kit into my schoolbag thinking, *Today's gonna be a good day.*

Jumping off the bus, I suddenly remembered that I didn't want to bump into Carmella at the main school entrance, so I headed for the side gate. I wanted to avoid her until I'd achieved my new plan of B-ball stardom.

Oh, for the life of Yoda!

Standing at the side gate was Brian Broxslater. He was chewing gum and leaning against the meshed fencing. His school tie was fat and his shirt cuffs were pulled over his jacket sleeves. His long brown hair reached his shoulders. He was wearing brand-new trainers. His thick legs seemed to be about to burst from his trousers, all Hulk-like. His eyes ignored everybody else and were trained on me. An evil grin escaped from the corners of his mouth. His moustache twitched. Beside him was his second-in-command – the skinny Corrington Wingburter with his pale, ghostly face.

I stopped in my tracks, but Broxslater's eyes never left me. I really should've hot-footed it outta there, but I decided that I'd rather pay my tax quietly than have Broxslater chase me around the school sports field.

"I heard you sold two insults yesterday," Broxslater said in a calm voice. His moustache danced. His fangs ripped into his chewing gum.

"Er, kind of—" I started to say.

"What do you mean 'kind of'?" Broxslater cut me off. "You either sold two cusses or you didn't. My spies tell me you sold 'em."

"Er, yeah, I did," I admitted.

"Then that's sixty p tax for the Chancellor," Broxslater demanded, holding out his hand. "Come on, Blakey, be a good soldier and pay the Chancellor."

Suddenly, a tiny Luke Skywalker appeared on my shoulder. Only I could see him. *Are you going to take that?* Luke said. *When are you going to stand up for yourself? You can't let him scare you for ever. Are you a mouse or a Jedi?*

Broxslater had massive fists. I imagined them pounding me into the ground up to my neck.

I thought about it. I chose being a mouse again.

Corrington laughed as I fished in my pockets for my jingles. I was grateful that Broxslater hadn't yet heard of my higher prices. I handed the money over and Broxslater's moustache twitched again as he pocketed my hard-earned cash.

"Now, be a good soldier and run along, Blakey," Broxslater laughed. "You don't wanna be late for registration."

This tiny ball of mad anger was ping-ponging side to side in my chest. It was being chased by this bigger ball of fear. Like a basketball, but much heavier. Very quickly, the gigantic ball of fear crushed the teeny ball of anger.

*

I made registration with five minutes to spare. As soon as I sat down, Harry Stanley started his performance. He had obviously been waiting for me. In between acting like a zombie, he made retching and vomiting sounds. He also came out with a new rhyme:

Hip hip, hip hip, Blakey's gonna be sick

Hip hip, hip hip, Blakey's gonna be sick

Duck down low

If you're sitting in the back row

Turn your face

Or it'll be covered in food waste

Get out of the way, you don't wanna be hit

*He puked over Karen Francis and she
had a proper fit*

Standing up to face him you must not dare

*Karen Francis is still brushing sick out
of her hair*

Hip hip, hip hip, Blakey's gonna be sick!

I tried to ignore him, but the roars of laughter encouraged Harry Stanley to go for an encore. My situation was tragic, but I couldn't help but admire Harry's lyrical skills.

"Hip hip, hip hip, Blakey's gonna be sick—"

"Harry Stanley!" my form tutor, Mr Gable, called out.

I hadn't seen him enter the classroom, but I breathed a sigh of relief as he sat down behind his desk.

The classroom calmed down and Gable started to read out the names in his register. I was third on the list. "Welton Blake!"

"Here!" I responded.

A second after I answered, Harry fell off his chair in mock agony and pretended to be kicked and punched from all sides. "Leave me alone," he squealed. "Leave me alone! I don't fight girls! Ouch! Ouch! Ouch! I don't fight girls!"

The classroom erupted once more and the only thing I could do was bury my face into my desk. I could hear pockets of giggles all around and when I did lift my head a bit and opened my eyes, everybody still chuckled – apart from Coral Chipglider. Her eyes narrowed as she glared at me. She was staring as if I had puked in her hair every day for a month. *Whatever did I do to her?* I made a note to myself: stay out of Coral's spitting range.

*

When the bell went, I hot-stepped to the music room for my first lesson of the day. The class had settled into their seats and the only free chair was the one next to Timothy "Stink Bomb" Smotheram. Today he had a mushroom, garlic and fishy smell about him. There was a mini snowstorm of dandruff on his shoulders and his lips had turned blue after chewing the wrong end of a biro. Despite all this, he grinned a strange grin.

"Blakey!" he greeted me. "Glad you're sitting here. Wanna ask you a favour. I need another insult."

"What? Another one?" I replied.

"Yeah, I need a smelly cuss."

"Why?" I asked.

"Because the girl I cussed said I smell like a Slumdog Millionaire toilet that even the ghetto kids won't use."

"That's deep," I sympathised.

"It was deep." Timothy nodded. "And nasty. Have you got something I can use? I'm desperate. This girl's a real pain on my ear lobes and knows her cusses."

"Let me think about it," I said. "By the way, my insults are now retailing for seventy pence."

"Seventy pence? What crook worked out your inflation? You're taking the double mickey."

"I don't care if I'm taking the treble mickey. Seventy pence."

"Why?" Timothy asked.

"Cos word got out to Broxslater about my insults yesterday and he taxed me this morning."

There was a guilty look on Timothy's face. My Jedi powers told me that Broxslater attempted to tax Timothy, who told him he'd given the last of his money to me.

"All right, I'll pay the seventy pence," Timothy said. "But the cuss better be one of your best. I don't want any D-minus cuss – it has to be A plus. I want tears on the floor."

"Don't worry, it'll be a business-class cuss," I told him. "And when I sell the insult, please keep it to yourself."

"All right."

"Promise!" I insisted.

"I promise," Timothy agreed.

I couldn't remember if I had a smelly cuss in my catalogue, so I had to make up one. I also thought that Timothy might help his cause by having the odd shower. "Tell her ... tell her she smells even worse than the armpit of a rhino who scrubs out the toilets in the rhino jail. Yeah, tell her that."

Timothy's eyes lit up. He wrote the cuss down and smiled an evil smile. Another satisfied customer. He paid me the seventy pence and I banked it in my right sock. "Remember," I said. "Keep this between me and you. Don't even tell your bedroom mirror. Broxslater must never know. We never had this conversation."

Timothy nodded and a bit of dandruff fell off his shoulders and onto his desk.

CHAPTER 10

The Secret Note

The morning classes passed in a boring blur and I managed to avoid Carmella. I still hadn't thought of a plan to avoid being lamed and shamed by her in public, so I spent lunch break in a corner in the library.

The book folk, the nerdy, the friendless and the weird kids all stared at me, but I didn't care. Broxslater wasn't taxing me, Harry Stanley wasn't rapping about my projectile vomiting and Coral Chipglider wasn't looking at me as if she wanted to drown me in an ocean of spit.

The buzzer sounded and I made my way to the next lesson of the day: Woodwork. I kept a careful look-out for Carmella in case I had to make a quick dash for it.

Suddenly, I was nudged in the back. I closed my eyes in dread, thinking it was Carmella. My knees went all funny and the inside of my head felt like someone was shovelling coal into it like it was one of those ancient train engines. For a moment I couldn't move. I slowly turned around, fearing the worst.

"Blakey! What's the matter with you?"

I breathed out a massive sigh of relief. It wasn't Carmella. It was Alice Stanbury. What could Alice Stanbury, one of the prettiest girls in my year, want with me? Maybe she was gonna tell me how tragic I'd looked when I jumped down the stairs and terminated my ankle. Her dimples weren't looking so cute.

"I was told to give you this," Alice said, passing me a folded piece of paper. "I'm not supposed to tell you who it's from, but it's definitely *not* me! You got that?"

I nodded. Before I went on my way, Alice put her hand on my arm and gripped it real tight. "Did you hear what I said? The message is *not* from me. If you say that it was, Bernice will be paying you a visit."

"OK, I get it," I said.

Alice marched off, looking back at me as if I'd broken into her bedroom and let Timothy Smotheram crap on her favourite dress. With everyone rushing around me, I stood still and opened the note. The writing was very small but neat. It read:

Meet me by the long-jump pit after school on Monday – C

The C had to be Carmella. I'd already given up any hope of taking her out this weekend and now I'd have to spend it worrying about meeting up with her on Monday. She was obviously tired of me avoiding her and wanted to officially end all interest in me. She would tell me she'd started to go out with Muscle Freak. I slowly folded up the note, banked it in my back pocket and made my way to Woodwork class.

I was the last one to arrive. Mr Cagney was at his table wearing an enormous pair of goggles. He was about to show us how to cut out a fish shape from a thin piece of pinewood. Our task for the lesson was to saw out the fish and stick it on this darker piece of wood. When we finished, we had to sand both bits of wood down and varnish the whole thing. I thought if I made a good job of it, I'd give it to my dad to hang up. He could do with looking at something other than the TV.

I decided to work on a bench in the corner, so I grabbed my wood and tools and hoped no one would bother me. A Polish kid, Gregorio Smolarek, was working at the bench next to me, but it was cool because he didn't chat too much. In fact, the only thing the Great Smo, as Gregorio was known, ever did say was, *"The English are soooo stooopid!"*

I was still thinking about the note that Carmella had sent me. *Meet me by the long-jump pit.*

It was possible that Carmella might invite all her friends to laugh at me. Everyone in town might be there, even the Mayor. Sky News might be in the ends. I could hear the reporter in my head. *Breaking news! We can confirm that Welton Blake has been officially rejected!*

Nicholas Fumbold skipped up to me and interrupted my thoughts. "Can I have another insult, Blakey?"

"Another cuss? Are you nuts?" I said. "I know you told Broxslater that I sold you a cuss. He taxed me this morning!"

"You sold an insult to Timothy today."

"How did you know that?" I asked.

Fumbold didn't answer.

"I'm not selling cusses," I insisted.

"You better," Fumbold warned me with a sneaky grin.

"You can't make me! As of today, I'm ending my insult business."

Fumbold moved closer to me. When his mouth was a centimetre away from my ear, he whispered, "If you don't sell me an insult, I'll let Broxslater know you sold a cuss today, and what's more, I'll tell him the cuss is about him. By the end of the day, Blakey, I think you'll be back in business."

I didn't answer Fumbold, but fear took hold of me. I was convinced Broxslater's fists could break mountains and karate chop pyramids. His neck was the same size as an oak tree trunk. And, of course, he had that moustache. From what I'd read, most of the evil people in world history had moustaches. Hitler, Mussolini, Fu Manchu, the Super Mario Brothers, Osama bin Laden, Dick Dastardly, Bernice Cummings' dad, Mr T in

Rocky 3 and this pizza delivery boy who always gave me a weird look. Broxslater could join that list and not be shamed. I'd look like an extra tomatoey pepperoni and olive pizza by the time Broxslater finished punching my face.

CHAPTER 11

Basketball Trial

My last lesson of the day was English with Miss Thomas. I found myself sitting worrying about how I would get home without Broxslater seeing me. Should I just find Carmella and get my rejection over with, rather than waiting till Monday?

In one half of my mind, Broxslater's fists were changing into Thor's hammer. In the other half, Carmella flew in a plane trailing a banner that said in massive red letters: REALLY SORRY, BLAKEY, I HAVE TO REJECT YOU COS I'M SOOO IN LOVE WITH MR MUSCLES.

Then it hit me. I had basketball practice after school. I didn't have to worry about escaping Broxslater's radar. I'd be making my way to the gym. Fumbold and Broxslater could be looking for me all over the place, but they'd never guess I was in the sports hall. This sudden thought made me smile.

After English ended, I hot-toed to the changing room next to the gym. Getting changed into blue shorts and a green vest was the captain of the B-ball team, Trevor Laing, along with the king of deodorant, Bruno Tardelli; the longest kid in our year, Philip Cribbins; and Gregorio Smolarek, the Great Smo. They were all bigger than me. I was proper glad to see Trevor there – he had a dob of kindness about him.

I was the last to get changed. I joined the others in the sports hall and Mr Purrfoot was waiting for us. He had a white sweatband around his head and was showing off a tight T-shirt which exposed his man-boobs. I was thankful that he was wearing tracksuit bottoms instead of his usual tight shorts.

Mr Purrfoot was bouncing a basketball and the sound it made echoed around the hall. "Where are Keith Hill and Valin Golding?" he asked.

"They weren't at school today, sir," Philip Cribbins replied.

"That's a shame," said Mr Purrfoot. "We have a game on Tuesday afternoon and we need to practise. We need ..."

Purrfoot suddenly noticed me. He stared at me for five seconds. I might as well have been an alien eating some weird munchies in that cadazy cantina in Mos Eisley in *Episode IV*. "Welton," Purrfoot managed after the shock had sunk in. "You ... you want to join the basketball squad?"

"Yes, sir," I said. "I've got zero ratings at cricket, football, running and hockey, so I thought I'd try basketball."

"That is splendid, Welton," Mr Purrfoot said. "I admire your enthusiasm."

Bruno Tardelli and Philip Cribbins chuckled. I don't think they admired my enthusiasm.

"It is not how good you are but the willingness to take part," Mr Purrfoot said, pointing a finger at everyone. "Let that be a lesson to you all. Welcome to the squad, Welton."

Mr Purrfoot's little speech made me feel a bit better.

I glanced at Trevor and he clenched his fist at me. "Go for it, Welton!" he yelled.

Everyone is good at something, I thought to myself. If I did all the training, I could be one of the best basketball players in the year in a month from now. Girls would be begging for me to go out with them. Carmella might be tempted to fire Muscle Freak and swap him for me. Alice Stanbury might give a damn about my ankle. The future looked all happy ever after.

"Right, follow me, lads," Mr Purrfoot ordered.

He led a variety of stretches to warm up, which ended with running on the spot. The sweat was pouring off me and I wondered when we were going to start practising with the ball. I didn't have long to wait. Purrfoot picked up the basketball and told us to stand in a circle. "Be alert," he said. "Catching practice!"

Purrfoot looked at Bruno Tardelli but threw the ball hard at the Great Smo. The Great Smo caught the ball easily and chucked it at Philip Cribbins. Philip tossed the ball over to me and I dropped it. Purrfoot shook his head, but Trevor encouraged me. "Come on, Blakey! Focus!"

"Welton is new to the squad, so let us go easy when we throw the ball to him," Purrfoot suggested.

Everyone passed the ball around at rapid speed until they moved it to me with a gentle lob. It wasn't the look I was going for.

After ten minutes, we began dribbling with the ball from one end of the court to the other. Purrfoot gave me the ball when it was my turn and said, "Take your time, son."

I did take my time, as I was going at about a quarter the speed of everyone else. But I managed to get to the other end of the court without losing control of the bouncing ball. I felt good! *Man! LeBron James? I can do what you do!*

"That was pretty good, son," Purrfoot remarked. "Next time, try to go a bit faster."

I felt even better when Philip Cribbins got himself in a tangle and fell over. I couldn't resist smiling to myself.

"Don't worry about it, Philip!" Trevor called out. "Better luck next time."

I could see why Trevor was the captain, because I was sure the rest of us were thinking, *What a clumsy clown!*

Gaining confidence, on my next turn I went a bit faster than my first run. Again, I kept control of the bouncing ball. When I got to the end, I even tried a shot into the basket. I was about two metres wide, but I heard encouragement behind me. Purrfoot was clapping politely.

"That's it, Blakey," Trevor shouted. "Next time try to compose yourself before the shot."

"Good effort, Welton," Purrfoot added. "Slow down a bit when you're preparing to shoot."

As I waited for my third turn, I imagined a crowd of Monks Orchard High fans clapping and cheering my shots into the basket. Carmella was among the spectators, with Muscle Freak. They were breaking up just as I scored another two points.

Philip Cribbins went next. After seven long strides the ball escaped him. He veered left, trying to rescue the situation, but stumbled and fell over again. The ball bounced down to the other end of the court. Purrfoot shook his head with his hands on his hips.

Trevor went to fetch the ball and passed it to me.

I took a few deep breaths. *Welton, time to bounce up the gears*, I told myself. I ran at full speed, bouncing the ball to the right of me. I was in control.

I glanced at the basket and ran towards it, still at full pelt. *This could be soooo awesome if I can shoot the ball into the hoop.* Then, out of the corner of my right eye, I saw a door open at the far end of the hall.

Carmella walked in. She instantly spotted me and sat down beside the door. My eyes returned to my task, but all I saw in front of me was a big white brick wall. I just couldn't stop myself. I didn't have any time to push out my arms to stop the crash. I kissed the white bricks with my forehead and dropped to the ground like a pancake sliding down a kitchen wall.

Everything went blurry. I think I blacked out for a while.

*

Something wet was on my forehead. My eyes opened. I found myself lying on my back staring at the lights hanging from the ceiling. Someone had placed a smelly towel under my head. It stank of toxic armpits. Four heads were looming over me: Mr Purrfoot, the Great Smo, Trevor Laing and Bruno Tardelli. I could smell Bruno's deodorant. Drops of my blood spotted the gym floor. My head felt like Darth Vader had used it for lightsaber practice.

"Don't move him," Purrfoot instructed. "We must wait for the ambulance. I have to call his parents."

As Purrfoot disappeared, the Great Smo said, "Why didn't you stop? I mean, how could you not see the wall? It's very biiiigggg. And white. You English are soooo stooopid!"

I looked around for Carmella, but she had disappeared.

*

The ambulance took me to Monks Orchard General Hospital. Just as the doctor finished inserting four stitches into my forehead, Mum arrived. As usual she went over the top, holding my face tenderly between her hands like I had been attacked by a mad bear. "Lord have mercy, Welton! They told me you had a fight with a wall?"

70

"I'm OK, Mum!" I said. "It's just a scratch."

Purrfoot told Mum what had happened. "Your son was performing his drills so well, but for some reason that I cannot explain, he ran into the wall."

"Thank you for staying with him, Mr Purrfoot," Mum said.

"That's all right, Mrs Blake. If Welton feels OK by Tuesday, I hope he can join the squad for the game. He'll have to wear a protective plaster or something."

"You want me to be in the squad for the game on Tuesday?" I said, not quite believing it.

"Yes, we do," said Purrfoot, smiling.

Suddenly, I felt a lot better. If my brain hadn't hurt so much, I would've got up and danced and done that sliding on the knees thing that footballers do after they score a great goal.

I wondered if I should write Carmella a note and tell her to meet me after the basketball game on Tuesday instead of on Monday. She wouldn't be able to resist me if I scored a spaceship load of points. And with stitches in my forehead, I'd look even cooler. The first stage of my mission to win back Carmella was in progress.

"You can be first or second substitute," said Trevor. "Philip Cribbins gets tired after about twenty minutes. He's clumsy, but because he's so tall he's useful. He's good at the tip-offs that start a game."

That was a bit of a downer, but I could still be the super-sub.

"Let's get you home," Mum said. I could tell she wanted to get out of the hospital as soon as possible. "Do you still want to go to your dad's tonight? You don't have to."

"Yeah," I replied. "He'll be expecting me."

CHAPTER 12

Dad

I climbed the concrete stairs to our flat with my brain still aching a bit.

"I have to say congratulations, Welton!" Mum said. "Making it to the squad of the school basketball team. That's a great achievement."

Mum made it sound like I had just been chosen out of one million hopefuls to play the lead role in a new *Star Wars* film. *If John Boyega can do it, then so can I.* She hadn't been this proud of me since I fried my first egg.

"I'm putting macaroni cheese in the oven," she said. "God knows if your dad will have anything to eat at his place."

"All right, Mum," I said. "I'm gonna crash."

I went to my room and looked in the mirror. I looked so cool with the stitches in my forehead. I tried a couple of bad-boy poses and reckoned Carmella wouldn't be able to resist me. Apart from his freakish body, what did Muscle Freak have that I didn't?

I packed a few clothes for my weekend stay with Dad, then lay on my bed waiting for my macaroni cheese, thinking about the basketball game next Tuesday.

*

After I'd eaten, Mum drove me to Dad's. She called him just before we left, so when we arrived outside his place, Dad was waiting for me on the pavement. He was still in his white working overalls and this grey cap specked with paint. I climbed out of the ride and went to open the boot to collect my bag.

"Welton," Dad called. "What's that?"

"What's what?"

"What happened to your forehead?"

"Oh, I had an accident at school playing basketball today," I explained. "I had to go to hospital to get it stitched up."

"You played basketball?" Dad asked. He sounded really surprised, as if I'd just beaten up ten Brian Broxslaters in a street fight.

"Yes, I did!" I said proudly.

"Come here," Dad said.

I went over to him and he studied my stitches like I was an expensive painting. "Angie!" Dad shouted to Mum. "Angie! Welton had an accident at school and you didn't tell me!"

"I didn't have time!"

Mum climbed out of the car. Dad was inspecting the rest of my head. "I'm his father! Don't I deserve to be told if something has happened to him? He's my son as well, you know. Or have you forgotten that? You treat me with utter contempt, Angie! I might not live with you any more, but I've got my rights—"

"I didn't have time to call you, Morris," Mum spat back at Dad. "I was at work when the school called me and I just rushed out to the hospital.

I'm sorry I didn't think of you, but I was worried if my son still had a head!"

"I should've been told!" Dad argued.

"And I should've been told when you started to have an affair with the accounts girl in your workplace!" Mum fired back.

I stood there shaking my head. I couldn't be bothered to stop them any more.

"That hasn't got anything to do with it!" Dad yelled.

"Hasn't it?! If you hadn't messed about with her, we could've driven to the hospital together!"

Dad was about to reply, but nothing came out of his mouth. He dropped his head.

Mum marched back to her car, slammed the door and drove off at *Fast & Furious* speed.

Taking my bag from me, Dad led me into his one-bedroom flat. He had recently painted the walls a creamy colour. My nose was itching from the paint fumes. His pile of movies beside the TV were a metre high. He had a three-seater sofa that folded out into a bed with a couple of giant cushions in the corners. There was a framed photograph of me in my school uniform on my first day at Monks Orchard hanging from a wall. The bin in his small kitchen was overflowing with takeaway cartons and kebab wrapping paper.

"Are you hungry, Welton?" Dad asked, opening his fridge and fumbling about in the freezer. "I've got some cheese flan and some fish-in-batter I can bung in the microwave."

I didn't want to tell Dad that Mum had already fed me because she didn't think he would have anything for me to eat.

"I'll have the fish-in-batter," I said.

"We can have some microwave chips with it," Dad said. "It'll make a sweet meal. I bet your mum thought I wouldn't have anything, right? Well, she's wrong. I went shopping in my lunch break. You can tell her that."

Before Dad placed the fish in the microwave, he switched on the TV and put on this ancient cowboy movie called *The Magnificent Seven*. I had seen the film about five times already, but Dad would get upset if I complained too much. *It's the greatest western ever made*, he always said. *It tells you everything you need to know about life.*

I still can't believe they killed off Charles Bronson's character.

So I waited for my second dinner of fish-in-batter and microwave chips while watching these poor Mexicans getting robbed and Yul Brynner doing his cool strut. The Seven were just setting off to face a zillion Mexican bandits with very bad moustaches when Dad served me my meal. The fish looked as dry as a cactus in a mad desert and the microwave chips were stuck to each other. I didn't complain.

Dad sat down beside me and started his meal.

"How's your mum?" he asked.

"She's all right," I answered.

I wondered if I should tell him about Greyback and the Brat moving in. I decided it was Mum's job rather than mine.

"I've ... I've been thinking, Welton ..." Dad said.

"What about?" I asked.

Suddenly, Dad looked proper sad. His top lip started to wobble. His eyes filled with tears. He turned away. Then he gazed at me.

I wasn't sure how to react or what to do. It was bad enough watching Darth Vader cry his guts out in *Revenge of the Sith*, but to see your own dad weeping was mega awkward. I couldn't move. I was speechless.

"I've been such a waste of space," said Dad, shaking his head and wiping his eyes. "I don't know what got into me. I suppose I thought the grass was greener on the other side of the fence. My mum always said I act first and don't stop to think."

I remained still as Dad went on. For some reason I thought it might be rude if I kept eating. A tear was falling down Dad's right cheek. I wanted to tell him to wipe it, but I couldn't. To me it looked like a waterfall.

"I'm going to make things right with your mum," Dad went on. "I've been living in a rut for too long. I want us to be all together again, living under the same roof. I realise I have to show her that I've changed."

Oh, Master Yoda, I thought. *The rolling credits on this one won't be good.*

"I love her, Welton," Dad went on. "Never stopped loving her. Love you too. Never forget that."

I really should tell him about Greyback, I thought. But what would Dad do if I did? He might just run into the window like that guy who was always committing suicide in *The Simpsons*. What would Obi-Wan Kenobi do in this situation? I didn't have a clue. Jedi Knights weren't exactly marriage counsellors.

"I want you back too," I managed to say.

Dad smiled, wiped away another tear and ate the rest of his food. I felt a bit better. I wondered who would win in a fight between Greyback and Dad. I'd put my money on Dad – Greyback was getting too ancient and rickety, and Dad might lick him with his extra-long paint-roller. I had to come up with funny stuff like that because it took me away from thinking about Dad crying.

CHAPTER 13

The Big Reveal

The next morning Dad was in a much better mood. He got up early to buy his newspaper. When he finished reading it, he offered to cut my hair. I agreed. Dad could always cut my hair better than Mum. With the stitches in my forehead and a good haircut, Carmella might change her mind about totally rejecting me.

"I got into the basketball squad, Dad," I said as he trimmed behind my ears.

"That's brilliant, Welton! Didn't even know you liked basketball?"

"Nor did I until I tried it. My first game's on Tuesday."

"I'll see if I can clock off from work early to watch," Dad said.

Yoda give me strength! I knew Mum would want to watch too and she'd be bound to bring Greyback and the Brat. I could be shooting some wicked hoops, but no one would take any notice because Dad would be mauling with Greyback on the sidelines. Everyone would laugh at me. Harry Stanley would write a new rhyme about my latest humiliation. Carmella might not reconsider going out with me because my family had too many issues.

"I don't want you to get in trouble at work, Dad," I said.

"Trouble? No, Welton. I'll just start early, say seven o'clock, take a half-hour lunch and leave at three thirty. No problem."

Oh, for the love of Luke! I really should tell Dad about Greyback and the Brat. I just didn't know how to start. What was I supposed to say? *Er, Dad, you know you said you wanted to get back with Mum? Well, er, that's not gonna happen cos Mum has got this new boyfriend who's really old and his son is the devil. And, er, they're moving in next week.*

"Have you got all the right gear for your game on Tuesday?" Dad asked now.

"Er, yeah," I said. "Got everything I need."

For a moment I was going to tell him that I needed new trainers, but I knew his budget wasn't well blessed lately. When he called Mum, all they did was argue about how much cash he should give her.

During our breakfast, Dad told me about his mission to set up his own painting and decorating company and his plans for our future as a family. "I took your mum for granted," he said. "Going out for drinks with workmates, blowing money in the bookies and not spending quality time with you guys. That won't happen again! No more! We'll be a team, more of a proper family unit. When I drop you off tomorrow night, I'm going to sit down with your mum and talk this all out."

Tiny Luke Skywalker appeared on my shoulder. He screamed into my ear and sliced into my skin with his lightsaber. *Tell him about Greyback and the Brat! Go on! What are you waiting for? Tell him before it's too late! Do you want your dad to feel more hurt than he does already?*

"Er, Dad," I said.

"Yes, Welton. What is it?"

I took a deep breath, sucking up all the air from my toes. Dad seemed so happy this morning. He looked better than I had seen him for a long time. He'd even had a shave. He was wearing jeans and a T-shirt that he had ironed earlier. I didn't want to delete that smile off his face. If anybody was going to do that, it had to be Mum.

"What are we going to do today?" I asked.

"What do you fancy?" he said. "Go to the leisure centre? Swimming? Bowling? Play some pool?"

I didn't want to tell him, but at twelve and a half years of age I was getting a bit too old to go swimming or bowling with my dad.

"Pool," I answered.

We drove to this pub called the Nine Mile Arms, about ten miles out of Monks Orchard. Dad led me into the pub and ordered a shandy for himself and a Coke for me. Luckily for us, the pool table was free. I felt like a proper man shooting pool with my dad that Saturday. We were laughing and joking as Dad showed me how to play trick shots and put backspin on the white ball.

When we arrived back at Dad's place, he let me play my *Call of Duty* game while he crashed. All the time I was wondering what would happen when Dad found out Mum's breaking news about Greyback and the Brat moving in.

*

The next morning, Dad convinced me to play table tennis with him at the Monks Orchard leisure centre. Again, he was in a good mood. Smashing the ball into my body made him laugh a lot. It was when we had a drink afterwards that I decided Dad must be told about Mum's drama.

"You want to get back with Mum, right?" I asked.

"Haven't you been listening to me all weekend, Welton?" Dad said, swallowing his beer. "Of course I do. There's nothing I want more."

"Can ... can I talk to her first?" I suggested.

"Welton, I'm sure I can do this myself. I mean, after all, I knew her before you were born. There isn't anybody alive who knows your mum better, apart from her parents maybe."

"She ... she might be interested in someone else," I said.

"Someone else? What are you saying?"

"Er, I'm not saying anything. Just that, er, Mum goes out a lot more now than what she used to."

"Goes out with who?" Dad asked. He leaned closer to me. "Who?"

Luke Skywalker appeared on my right shoulder again. He stamped his feet. He had a megaphone in his hands and he jabbed it into my ear. *Tell him now!*

I hesitated.

I looked up at Dad and thought of the good time we'd had over the weekend. I didn't want to be the one who burst his good-mood balloon.

"She ... she sometimes goes out with workmates," I said.

"She does, does she? Any workmate in particular?" Dad asked.

"Well, er, not a workmate."

Luke Skywalker was blazing me with his lightsaber. *TELL HIM!*

"He ... he's a security guard at the Orchard shopping centre," I blurted out.

The beer bottle in Dad's hand stopped just in front of his mouth. I could see him swallowing something, but it wasn't beer. Dad finally placed the bottle down on the table. "A security guard?" he repeated.

I nodded.

"She's seeing a security guard?" Dad said again, like I had to tell him ten times before he believed it.

I nodded again.

Dad looked around the cafeteria, trying to be calm.

"You all right, Dad?" I asked.

"Yeah, I'm fine," he said. "I mean, what did I expect? Can't expect her to stay single, can I? We split up some time ago. It's my fault for being so stupid."

I thought of the Great Smo.

"Sorry, Dad," I said.

"Not your fault. She should've told me, not you. So ... how long has your mum been seeing this security guard guy?"

"Er ... not sure," I lied.

"Have a guess?"

"Er, about five months."

"Five months?!" Dad yelped.

"Yeah, and, er ... he's moving in next week."

"Moving in?!"

Dad turned away. He gripped his hands and interlocked his fingers.

"You all right, Dad?" I said. "I just thought it was best to tell you. Didn't want you coming to my B-ball game and seeing them together."

"You've done the right thing, Welton," Dad said. "And your mum has the right to live the life she wants to live. But when I drop you off later, I still want a word with her."

"You're ... you're not gonna go cadazy and cuss the neighbours like you did last time?" I said.

"No, Welton. I've matured. I don't go crazy any more."

*

Dad was silent while he drove us back to his place. He'd spent time in his room as I played another game of *Call of Duty*. Just after two o'clock he came out and said, "We're leaving early today, Welton. Pack up your things."

"It's only just gone two, Dad," I pointed out.

"Remember I said I need to speak to your mum?"

I knew that Greyback and the Brat spent Sundays with Mum. She would usually cook dinner for them and they would go home about five o'clock, so they'd still be in the flat when Dad and I got there.

My heart boomed with surround sound. I tried to think of something to stop him. "You don't want to go swimming, Dad?" I asked.

"Wasn't table tennis enough exercise for you? No, I really need to drop you off and talk with your mum."

I took as long as I could to pack my overnight bag. I spent more than a minute placing it in the back of Dad's work van. When I sat in the passenger seat, I fiddled with the seatbelt. Dad gave me a long hard stare. I checked the time: 2.30 p.m. He turned the key in the ignition and pulled away.

When we arrived at my block, Dad lifted my bag from the back of his van and waited for me to lead him to my door. Normally, he would drop me off and drive home. Not today.

I turned the key in the front door. I checked behind me. Dad smiled at me. He was still on his best behaviour. Maybe he was too quiet.

I entered my flat. "Welton!" Mum called. "Is that you, Welton?"

"No, Mum. It's Jabba the Hutt. Of course it's me!"

"You're early, aren't you?" Mum said. "Did your dad have to go somewhere?"

I walked along the hallway with Dad behind me. Mum was in the kitchen. She was washing the dishes. The Brat played a Wii tennis game on the TV. Greyback sat in an armchair. He sipped a mug of coffee. The look on his face when he spotted Dad was just like Luke Skywalker when he saw Yoda for the first time. Greyback took in a breath and placed his mug down on the coffee table. Dad narrowed his eyes and stared at him the way a lion glares at a limping zebra.

"I ... I wasn't expecting you to bring Welton back so soon," said Mum.

"I need to talk to you in private," said Dad.

"I have guests, Morris," Mum said. "Can it keep?"

"No, it can't keep. It's about our future."

"What future, Morris?"

"What do you mean, what future?" Dad asked. "Our future, Angie."

"I'm not sure I know what you're talking about," said Mum. "Like ... like I said, I have guests. Can we discuss this another time?"

The Brat paused his game. Even he realised that something dramatic was going down. Greyback stood up.

"No! I don't want to talk about it another time," Dad insisted, looking at Greyback. "I want to talk about this now."

"Er, Welton," Greyback said softly. "Shall I help you take your bag to your room? I think your parents want some privacy. You come too, Devon."

"Don't you talk to my son!" Dad shouted at Greyback.

"I didn't mean any offence," said Greyback.

Dad rushed towards Greyback, pulled back his right arm and swung a right hook that connected with Greyback's jaw. It sent him flying over the coffee table. His ponytail danced in the air. The mug of coffee emptied itself all over the floor.

Dad was standing over Greyback, breathing like an angry Darth Vader. The Brat ran up to Dad and booted him in the leg. "Leave my dad alone!"

Greyback slowly got to his feet, rubbing his jaw.

"Get out! Get out!" Mum yelled at Dad. "Get out of my flat, Morris! Get out of my LIFE!"

Dad gazed at his bruised knuckles and glanced at Greyback. The Brat kicked Dad again. "Get out!" he squeaked. "Get out!"

I didn't know whether to laugh or cry.

Dad looked at me with sadness in his eyes. He then stormed out and slammed the door behind him.

"Never step in my flat again!" Mum screamed after him.

She went to tend to Greyback. The Brat looked at me like he wanted to play football with my shins too.

I didn't know whether to see if Dad was all right or to tell Mum that Dad only acted the way he did because he wanted her back. The Brat returned to his game and I decided to go to my room.

"Don't you turn out like your dad, Welton," Mum called to me. "He's always had a nasty temper. Lord knows how I found myself with him in the first place! What was I thinking?"

Mum's words were like hot coals dropped onto my heart. *He's my dad!* I thought. *Yeah, he has his issues and he's got a temper with it, but I don't*

get to choose another one. If Greyback moves in,
Dad is still my dad.

I fell onto my bed, closed my eyes and heard
Mum cursing Dad's name for the rest of the
afternoon.

CHAPTER 14

An Unexpected Meeting

Mum was still going on about Dad's meltdown the next morning, but all I could think about was meeting Carmella by the long-jump pit later on. Today was the day I was going to get officially terminated.

When I arrived at school, I didn't go up to the gates until I checked to see if Broxslater and Corrington Wingburter were collecting their morning taxes. They weren't.

I managed to get to registration without seeing Carmella. If she was going to shame me, I only wanted to see her once today.

As Mr Gable took the register, I spotted Harry Stanley bursting to give another rap performance. Others were shouting him on. "Go for it, Harry!"

"Welton Blake?" Mr Gable called.

"Here!" I answered.

That was Harry's cue. I kind of expected it. There was no way I could've kept my running into the gym wall a secret. To be honest I felt lucky that nobody had filmed it on their mobile phone and posted it up on YouTube.

Blakey, the fool, went to play basketball

For all his days, he's never been cool

Not even Z-list chicks fancy him

Blakey playing B-ball should be a mortal sin

He can't catch, he can't run

He can't even beat a nun in a fun run

He can't jump, he can't shoot

He doesn't know where the buttons go on a three-piece suit

He's not very tall

To shoot a basket he needs to stand on a stool

He might now be blind, concussed and all

After his forehead kissed the freakin' brick wall.

The whole class collapsed in giggles. Two of Harry's mates rolled on the floor. Even the quiet students were laughing like cadazy. Mr Gable turned his back on the class for a private chuckle.

The only person who wasn't amused was Coral Chipglider. She was wearing this black make-up I had never seen on her before. She looked like she wanted to drown everyone in the school with her spit. "Shut up!" she yelled, glaring at Harry Stanley, Mr Gable and me. The classroom went quiet, especially those who were within spitting range.

"Thank you," Mr Gable said to Coral.

"They're so immature," Coral said. "Can't they grow up?"

Mr Gable resumed registration. Harry Stanley made faces at me. He looked seriously disappointed he didn't get to rap a second verse. Coral stared at me as if she wanted to decorate my face with brown slime from the local swamp.

I couldn't work out why Coral had stood up for me. Maybe I had found the only person in the galaxy who felt sorry for me.

*

I managed to lie low for the rest of the day, which seemed to drag on for ever. But finally it was time for me to meet up with Carmella.

As I crossed the school playing fields, I looked into the far corner. There was nobody near the long-jump pit. Maybe Carmella had taken pity on me, I thought. Maybe she decided I had been humiliated enough over the past few days. I headed for the pit anyway. I'd give it ten minutes to see if she turned up.

After reaching the pit, I sat down and looked around. I felt lonely. I thought about Dad and realised he was never going to come home and live with us. I had a strange feeling in my stomach again.

Looking around, I spotted a figure coming out from the back of the school. It was a female student. She was alone. I stood up. She was walking across the football pitch towards me.

I took five steps forward. The sun was in my eyes as I peered into the field. It wasn't Carmella. I knew Carmella's walk off by heart.

Oh, by the power of Yoda! It couldn't be! This can't be happening ... It was Coral Chipglider. The note was in my pocket. I took it out. It was signed with a big C. *Oh no!* The C must've stood for Coral, not Carmella. I thought I was going to have a heart attack. *Do twelve-and-a-half-year-old boys suffer heart attacks?*

Coral was only thirty metres away. She wasn't smiling. She spat on the ground. Maybe she had put on her black make-up to perform some demon-worship killing. Maybe I was her sacrifice. My brain told me to run like a Jamaican. Something else instructed me to wait and see what she had to say.

Coral stepped right up to me. I didn't think she had ever smiled in her life. Even if a hundred comedians turned up at her birthday party and tickled her with their tickling sticks, I still didn't think she'd bust a grin.

"Blakey," Coral greeted me. She was wearing a long blue skirt and stacked shoes that made her taller than me. She spat into the pit. It looked disgusting on the sand. "You might be wondering why I sent you the note."

"Er, yes," I said, nodding.

She still wasn't smiling. "Because I like you," Coral said. "Kinda feel sorry for you in a way. Everybody takes the double mickey out of you. But I like you. You're funnier than Harry Stanley. I've heard some of your insults. They're hilarious. You're black too. I find that really interesting. You're an outsider like me."

"Er, thank you, Coral," I said.

"So, are we gonna stand up here like two stale turds or are you gonna walk me home?" Coral asked.

"Er, I'll walk you home."

She polluted the pit with her spit again. This time there was a bit of red in the sticky, bubbly goo. My stomach did a double rinse like a washing machine.

Coral made for the school exit and I caught up with her. Her dark eyes looked straight ahead when she spoke. She had long brown curly hair. I didn't think she brushed it that often. She had strange silver rings on her fingers. One was a skull and another was a dragon.

"My mum's a dentist," Coral said. "She does all the rich people's teeth. Boring, she is. I call her 'Miss Salmon'. That's what Mum leaves me for my dinner. I'm sick of salmon!"

"I ... I don't like it too much either," I said.

"She has boring friends who always come around," Coral continued. "They talk about their boring house extensions, their boring gardens and what they grow in their boring greenhouses."

She suddenly stopped walking, turned and looked at me. "They make me feel like sawing off my ears. I can't take it any more!"

Coral resumed walking. Her eyes were focused ahead, like two headlights on a long, straight motorway. "My parents used to give me birthday parties every six months. With a pink cake I had to cut. I hate pink! Who has birthday parties every six months? I hated them!"

"I've ... I've never had a birthday party ..." I said.

I started to think that I was walking home with someone who might torture koala bears in their spare time. If she didn't kill me, I thought I might ask her to babysit the Brat. He'd never misbehave again.

"You're not missing anything," Coral went on. "My parents always invited the children of their boring friends. They drank boring wine. They don't know I started to drink their wine."

"Er … you drink wine?" I managed.

"Course!" Coral replied. "I drank some of the expensive ones that Dad keeps in the cellar. I know where he hides the key. Maybe Dad does know. He's probably too scared to tell me off about it."

"I've … I've never had wine before …" I said.

"We'll have to change that, Blakey. As I said, I like you. You're different, not one of the normal Monks Orchard boring kids. I hate it here! We're gonna make a good team. We're gonna rock this boring world. I'll teach you how to snog."

"Er, snog?" I squeaked. Suddenly, my cheeks felt like hot grills.

"You ever curled tongues with a girl before, Blakey?" Coral asked.

I wanted to answer yes, but Coral would probably know I was lying. "Er ... no."

"Then I'll be the one to teach you," she said.

"That'll be good. Thanks."

Something inside me squirmed.

"Soon we'll run away from this boring place," Coral said. "Go to the city! Somewhere dangerous like South Crongton."

Coral's brain was obviously nuttier than a jar of Nutella, but I kind of liked the idea of running away. But not with Coral. Why couldn't Carmella or Alice make me the same offer? If they did, I'd give it some proper consideration.

We walked uphill to the part of Monks Orchard filled with 4x4 people-cruisers. We had a good view of the fields and the town from the gaps between the houses. Some homes had three rides in their driveways. Foreign nannies pushed buggies with kids in them that really should've been walking. One old guy was playing soldiers with tiny plastic men on his lawn. He even had toy tanks and cannons. Coral joked about how she was planning to kidnap the whole little army one night. She kept on saying how cool it'd be if we lived in Crongton.

Suddenly, I saw Carmella. She was on the other side of the road with a friend. I think my heart dropped into my stomach and split into pieces as it made its way down to my knees. My head felt like it was on fire.

I slowed down. Carmella stopped and looked across. At least if Coral kept me hostage in her wine cellar for a week, Carmella could say to the police she saw me with someone.

Carmella's eyes met mine. As she recognised me, her face seemed to change into a giant question mark. *What in the name of Yoda are you doing with crazy Coral Chipglider?*

I wanted to run across the road and explain everything, but Coral might go cadazy. I'd had enough of mad girls giving me the smackdown in the past week.

Carmella set off in the opposite direction. She looked behind once as she walked five paces, then she stopped and glanced backwards again. I couldn't call Carmella's name. I couldn't even take a step in her direction. My cheeks were so hot they could sizzle a buffalo wing.

"Keep up, Blakey!" Coral ordered. "What are you slowing down for? I wanna get home by this afternoon not tomorrow morning! Come on! We've got some snogging prep to do."

My head was telling me to hot-leg it all the way home, but there was something compelling about Coral. We steadily walked uphill and turned into another road.

Coral pointed to her house.

There were two stone eagles each perched on a pillar of marble at the entrance of Coral's driveway. I saw a jeep, a sports car and a Mercedes. Han Solo could've landed the Millennium Falcon on the front lawn and there would still be room to swing a few giraffes.

"Nobody's home," Coral said. "Mum and Dad are still at work. The gardener goes home at four. You wanna come in? There's a cinema room in the basement with surround sound. I've got loads of horror movies."

"Er, I would, but I promised to see my dad," I lied. "I'm late already."

"Why would you step all the way up to my house if you knew you had to leave straight away?"

I had to think fast. "Er … I wanted to be polite. And you're … interesting."

"Interesting? Is that all?"

"That's … that's a lot. So many girls at our school are boring."

"Hmmmm."

"Next time I'll stay longer," I promised.

Coral grinned. "Before you go, I give you permission to kiss me," she said.

"Kiss you?"

"Yeah, you wanna learn, right?" Coral asked.

"Er … yeah."

"Well, come here then! I ain't gonna eat you."

"Slurp tongues with you now?" I said. "What about the prep? You're not gonna write down what I need to do? You know, like in science, where you have to write down the method or something?"

"No, Blakey," Coral said. "This isn't a chemistry lesson. We're going straight into the practical. You have to learn sometime."

I took two steps towards her. Coral gazed at me before spitting on the ground. She wiped her lips with the back of her hand. I wiped mine with the sleeve of my school blazer. Her eyes looked like the secret burial place for Harry Potter spiders.

Suddenly, Coral reached out her arm and pulled my head towards hers. She locked her lips on mine. It was like being kissed by a rubber doughnut. I didn't really do anything. She closed her eyes and sort of made a snack out of my lips. It was like eating jelly. You didn't bite jelly. You just sort of sucked it in. I pulled away. I could taste mint chewing gum and custard creams.

"What's the matter, Blakey?" Coral asked.

"Nuh ... nuh ... Nothing's a matter. It's just ... just I'm interested in someone else."

"Who?" Coral demanded.

"Car ... Car ... Carmella McKenzie," I blurted out. "I've fan ... fancied her for ages."

Coral gave me a long hard stare. I braced myself for a massive greenie to splat on my face. I closed one eye and squinted the other. I prayed that when Coral killed me, Yoda would grant me a second life as a spirit.

Coral turned her back on me and opened her front door. She turned around and narrowed her eyes. "If she upsets you, Blakey, it's me and her!" Coral said. "One of us will no longer be able to do our eye make-up in the mornings ... and it won't be me."

Something icy and jagged ran down my spine. I wished I had made friends with Coral before. Broxslater would've never picked on me.

Coral went inside and slammed the door. I had to sit down because my knees were wobbling. I think I was suffering from shock. I breathed out hard and thanked Yoda I was still alive. A minute later, I left Coral's place. I thought she was watching me from an upstairs window, so I didn't run.

CHAPTER 15

A Gift

As I walked further away from Coral's mansion, I stepped faster and faster. I made it back to where I'd last spotted Carmella, but she was gone. I went into the nearest shop and bought a bottle of water. I washed out my mouth and walked across town to my dad's place. I pressed his doorbell but heard nothing from inside. His van was parked on the street. I thumbed his doorbell again. I heard steps.

The door opened. Dad was still wearing the same clothes he'd had on yesterday. He was unshaven and looked like he had been sampling something stronger than shandy. "Welton," Dad said. "Didn't expect to see you today. You should've told me you were coming around."

"My mobile doesn't work," I told him.

I followed Dad inside. Oh my days. The Death Star had exploded. There was a new red stain on the wall of his living room. His movies were scattered all over the floor. There were bits of a smashed glass in the corner. A dinner plate lay shattered next to the fridge.

Dad made his way to the sofa. He was watching a western. "Sit down. Make yourself at home."

I didn't sit down. As Dad watched his movie, I swept up the broken glass and plate and tidied up. When I'd finished, Dad gave me a sad look. "Sorry, Welton. Don't think I'm too good at dealing with bad news. I took everything out on my place."

"Yeah you did," I said. "Can't give you any ratings on how you deal with stuff."

"I didn't go to work today," Dad said. "I called in sick."

I parked beside him. Dad shifted over a bit. His breath stank of wine. There was a bit of sofa fluff in his hair. "Greyback might be moving in, but you're still my dad," I told him.

"What do you call him?" Dad asked.

"Er, Greyback."

Dad started to roar with laughter. He rolled off the sofa and bumped his head, but he carried on chuckling. I giggled with him.

"Greyback!" Dad yelled. "I lost my wife to Mr Greyback! Well, thank you very much, Mr Greyback!"

We cracked up for another ten minutes. It was why I liked my dad so much. He was a grown-up, but sometimes he could be like a big kid.

Before I left, I asked him, "Are you coming to watch me tomorrow?"

"Of course," Dad said. "Miss out on my son playing basketball? Could never do that, Welton."

"Oh, Dad," I called. "Mum said that if you even think about coming into our flat again, she's gonna lick you with the plant pot."

Dad chuckled again. "I wouldn't have it any other way," he said. "When I pick you up the next time, tell her I'll be waiting in the van. And tell Greyback I'm sorry."

I left Dad's place in a good mood. Maybe I could boost him up more if I set him up with a date. This was one of my better ideas. After all, Mum had Greyback. Why shouldn't Dad have someone? I was sure Yoda would approve.

I could try to find out what kids in my year have single mums. *Yeah, that'll be my next mission. But I'll have to find out what they look like. I don't want my dad linking with a Z-class slummy mummy. Alice Stanbury's mum must have good looks ratings. I'll try to get some facial recognition on her.*

I made it home just after seven. Mum wanted to know where I'd been. Greyback and the Brat were also there.

"I went around to see Dad," I told Mum. Greyback turned to look at me. "He ... er ... said sorry," I added.

"So he should," said Mum. "Wash your hands before I give you dinner. I've got a surprise for you later on."

"What surprise?" I asked.

Could it be Carmella wrapped up in the flat somewhere ready to agree to be my girlfriend? Didn't think so.

"Once you wash your hands and eat your dinner, you'll find out!" Mum said.

After dinner, Mum disappeared for a couple of minutes to get something from her room. She returned carrying a box. She placed it on the kitchen table where I was sitting. She was smiling like a kids' TV presenter. It was a new phone!

"For me?" I asked.

"Of course it's for you!" Mum said. "I don't see any other twelve-year-old boys lacking a phone in my flat. Do you?"

"No, Mum. Mega thanks! I can't believe it. Thanks with a big T."

I stood up, almost knocked my glass over and gave Mum a hug as if I'd just come back from a mad war.

"By the way," Mum said. "Devon and his dad are moving in next Saturday. The new bed's coming on Thursday. We're going to be a new family."

Mum clapped her hands together. Greyback kissed her on the cheek. The Brat was bouncing up and down on an armchair shouting, "And we're going on holiday together. We're going to the sea, sea, sea, how about me, me, me!"

"We're going on holiday?" I asked. In my mind I could see myself burying the Brat up to his neck in sand as the tide came in.

"Er, yes, Welton," Mum replied.

"Where to?"

"We haven't decided yet," Mum answered.

I sort of half-smiled. Going on holiday with Mum, Greyback and the Brat? Maybe I could do that? I could ask for my own room. I might even ask if we could go to Morocco, where they shot scenes for the *Star Wars* movies.

For the rest of the evening I tried to be as polite as I could. After all, I did have my new phone. I even let the Brat beat me at Connect Four. He wasn't that bad when he wasn't bouncing on my bad leg. "I'm your little brother now," he said after the game.

I took it in. "Yes, you are," I replied.

I'm your little brother. Those words stayed with me for the rest of the night. *Maybe I could use my Jedi powers and turn the Brat to the good side*, I thought. *Yeah, that's a plan. In a matter of days I could send him to the shops for me and get him to clean my room.*

Before I crashed that night, I pulled out the SIM card from my dead phone and placed it in the new one. I closed my eyes and made a quick prayer to Yoda. *It worked!* I added all my phone contacts into my new mobile. I suddenly realised I didn't have many numbers. I had my parents' details and a few more relatives. There were a couple of mates that I'd left behind in Ashburton. I used to text them every day, but that'd changed into a text a month. The only contact I had at school was Carmella. How sad was that? Was I really that unpopular? The only girl to ever take a real interest in me was Coral Chipglider.

It was half past ten. I stared at Carmella's phone number with my thumb hovering over the little green phone icon. I desperately wanted to ask her why she started to go out with Muscle Freak and didn't tell me. Maybe she didn't tell me because she never saw me as boyfriend material. Any bravery I had grew long legs and hot-toed

away from me. I switched my phone off and
placed it on my bedside cabinet.

CHAPTER 16

The Game

After school the next day, it felt good to pull on the green vest and blue shorts of our basketball team. Trevor Laing came up to me and wished me luck. My other team-mates, including Valin Golding and Keith Hill, ignored me.

Mr Purrfoot entered the changing room wearing a new tracksuit. It was loose-fitting so you couldn't see his man-boobs. He was also showing off a white headband over a new haircut. "Come on, lads!" he said. "Look sharp! Wake up! It's time."

Trevor got us into a huddle. He screamed, "Are we ready to B-ball?!"

"YES, WE'RE READY TO B-BALL!" we replied.

It really felt good to be part of all this. Now I knew how the mighty Chewbacca felt to be tagging along with Luke Skywalker, Princess Leia, R2-D2, C-3PO and Han Solo.

I followed my team out of the changing room and into the gym. Cheers echoed around the hall. There were about fifty spectators, three of them being Mum, Greyback and the Brat. There was no sign of Dad.

The team we were playing was Biggin Spires Tech, a school from a town about fifteen miles away. Their players were all wearing identical basketball socks, shorts and sweatbands. They even had numbers on the backs of their purple vests. Their kit looked many ratings better than our basic green vests and blue shorts. We all glanced at each other, very worried.

Their PE teacher started the game. He was dressed in a proper referee's shirt. I sat on the substitute's bench with Bruno Tardelli and Mr Purrfoot. Every two seconds Purrfoot leapt up in the air as if he was sitting on a bucket full of piranhas. He complained about everything. The referee ignored him and that made Purrfoot scream and jump even higher. Every so often I glanced into the crowd. When Mum saw me, she smiled.

Then I spotted Carmella. Muscle Freak was with her.

They sat on the floor in the corner with their backs against the wall. At first, I tried to pretend I hadn't seen them. But I couldn't help myself. The insides of my stomach felt like there was a tiny mouse going cadazy with a pair of scissors. I watched them more than the game. At least Muscle Freak didn't have his arm around her. I thanked Yoda he wasn't kissing her. That would've killed me.

I lost track of the score as I spied on Carmella and Muscle Freak for the next fifteen minutes. Mr Purrfoot had taken to the sidelines of the court shouting instructions, but he suddenly yanked my arm. "Welton! You're on!"

I looked into the crowd. Mum and Greyback were on their feet clapping. On the opposite side to them, I spotted Dad. He was still in his work overalls. His paint-specked hat was pulled over his eyebrows. He clenched his right fist and yelled, "Go on, Welllltttonnn!"

Everyone heard Dad. They all looked around.
Mum side-eyed Dad and half-grinned. I couldn't
help but smile, a warm feeling in my stomach. I
kept on saying to myself, *Don't run into the wall,
don't run into the wall, don't run into the wall.*

Mr Purrfoot pulled me close to him and
whispered in my ear. "Don't try any fancy tricks
or moves. When you get the ball, try to pass it on
to one of the other boys. That's all I want you to
do … Oh, one last thing. Look where you're going.
Let's not have another wall incident."

"All right, sir," I said.

I suddenly realised I didn't know what the
score was. Behind one of the baskets, a Year
Seven kid was operating a manual scoreboard.
We were losing 26 points to 30.

My first touch of the ball was tragic – Bruno
Tardelli passed me an easy ball and I dropped
it. One of the opposing players collected the ball,
jet-heeled down to the basket and scored.

Trevor Laing ran up to me. "Focus," he said.
"Keep your eye on the ball and try to ignore the
crowd."

I nodded. I glanced at Carmella, then looked away.

My next bit of action was slightly better. I managed to catch the ball after our opponents had tried to score. I pushed out a quick pass to the Great Smo and after a few more passes, Trevor scored. To hear the crowd cheering was brilliant. And I had played my part. Everyone clapped, including Carmella and Muscle Freak.

I started to relax. I never tried to do too much. I just kept on passing the ball to my team-mates.

Two minutes to go. Biggin Spires were leading 46 to 45. Mr Purrfoot's face had turned red. He looked like he was about to give birth to a giant basketball. My legs were tiring. My vest was sticking to my back. Sweat was dripping between my eyelashes.

One of their players had attempted a long shot. It bounced on the edge of the basket but didn't go in. Trevor made a mighty leap and caught the rebound. He tried to get a pass to Valin, but he was tightly marked. Trevor passed to me. I caught the ball and went down-court.

Purrfoot was going proper bonkers, yelling, "Pass to Valin! Pass to Valin!" I made sure I stopped well before the brick wall. I looked up, ready to give a pass.

I couldn't quite get the ball to Valin, so I bounce-passed to Bruno Tardelli. He had two defenders blocking his progress, so he threw the ball to the Great Smo. Catching the ball easily, the Great Smo lined up a shot, but a defender parried the ball and it headed towards me. Time was running out. The crowd were on their feet.

"Pass to Valin! Pass to Valin!" Purrfoot screamed.

The referee glanced at his stopwatch. Out of the corner of my eye I spotted Carmella and Muscle Freak jumping up and down. The ball was in my right hand. The referee gripped his whistle. He sucked in a big breath. He prepared to blow. I sort of bowled the ball towards the basket. It hit the backboard and bounced heavily on the rim. All eyes were on the ball. The crowd hushed. I noticed Dad running forward to get a closer look. Mr Purrfoot watched with his mouth open. Purple veins suddenly appeared on his cheeks.

The ball rolled on the rim ... and dropped into the basket. I couldn't believe it! Forty-seven points to us! The Great Smo jumped on my back. Trevor Laing leapt onto my shoulder. Bruno sprang onto my other arm. Valin dived on top of my head. I collapsed under the weight.

By the time I got up, the game was over. We had won by one point. Clapping and cheering rang in my ears. Dad ran onto the court. He almost knocked me over before lifting me up, shouting, "Welllltttonnn!"

It was kind of embarrassing to be picked up like that, especially in front of Carmella. Mr Purrfoot wasn't too happy with Dad running on the court in his work boots. Dad returned to the sidelines after Purrfoot gave him a filthy look.

We shook hands with our opponents. I could feel this hot glow in my chest. *Oh, sweet Yoda!* It felt good. I went over to Mum at the side of the court. I hoped she wasn't gonna give me a super mum-hug in front of everyone, but she did. What was worse, she kissed me on the forehead. *Luke Skywalker! Can you hear me? Will my humiliations never end?* I wondered. Greyback was there too. He shook my hand. "That was brilliant, Welton."

I had tried to hate Greyback from the first day I saw him, but now? I just couldn't. He was … well, all right. I just hoped he wouldn't die too soon and upset Mum.

Just as I was heading to the changing room, Carmella walked onto the court.

I waited for her. I shifted from foot to foot. My heart pumped harder than it had during the game.

Muscle Freak remained where he was. Maybe he was feeling sorry for me. It would've been too much if he was here to listen to what Carmella had to say.

"That was so cool, Welton," she said. "I didn't know you could play B-ball?"

She called me Welton! I wanted to kiss her just because of that.

"I … I can't," I replied. "It was a lucky shot."

"Don't put yourself down," Carmella said, taking a step closer to me. "For your first game I reckon you were on the boards, man!"

I blushed. Good job I had a chocolate complexion otherwise I would've gone redder than Dracula's blood sample.

"I saw you practising the other day," Carmella said. "You, er … had an accident."

"Er, yeah. Had issues with the wall."

Carmella laughed. Unlike Coral, she hadn't got any custard-cream crumbs in her mouth. "I was the one who called the ambulance," Carmella revealed.

"You?" I said.

"Yes, me. I called them on my mobile when you were knocked out. Purrfoot asked me to."

"Oh, er … thanks."

"That's all right. I was trying to catch up with you all week," she said.

Oh, Yoda, my green holiness. Here it comes. She's going to announce her wedding plans to Muscle Freak.

"Oh?" I replied. "What did you want to see me about?"

"Our date, stupid. Don't tell me you've forgotten? Weren't we meant to go to the movies?"

"But, er, what about ...? We were? Er, what about ...?"

I was very confused. I glanced at Muscle Freak standing about five metres behind Carmella. He was chewing something that made the muscles in his neck bulge out like rocks in a pair of skinny tights. I imagined him headbutting me and breaking my nose. Carmella glanced behind her and started to laugh.

"I ... I don't think it's funny," I said. "You can't go out with him *and* me."

She kept on laughing. She was holding her belly. She bent over. "That's ... that's Sheldon. Sheldon Manley. He's ... he's ..."

"He's what? Your new boyfriend? I kind of guessed that, Carmella."

"No! No!" she said. "He's my cousin. He's just moved in with us from North Crongton. His parents wanted him to move out from there. He was getting into too much trouble and drama.

He's new to the school, so I've been showing him around."

"Your cousin?" I replied. "Why … why didn't you say?"

"I tried to. I tried calling you. No answer. Every time I saw you, you ran off … By the way, what were you doing with Coral Chipglider?"

"Er … I, er."

"You're not going out with her, are you?" Carmella asked.

"No! Course not. I was just walking her home …"

"She's a bit cadazy. We all stay away from her. Even the teachers don't mess with her."

"She … she wanted to show me her house," I explained. "Massive it is. Her front garden's as big as a football pitch."

"What else did she show you?"

I couldn't help but think of Coral's kiss. "Er … nothing … she showed me nothing."

Carmella didn't look convinced. "Hmmmm."

"I didn't stay at her place for long," I said.

"So she showed you around her mansion, did she?"

"Not really."

"Hmmmm," Carmella said again. "I think you tickle her fancy."

"Er ... don't know about that," I replied.

"She didn't try anything with you?" Carmella wanted to know.

"Nope."

"Hmmm?"

Carmella gave me a Judge Judy look.

"That's all," I said. "Coral and me haven't got anything going on."

"So she won't pollute me with her gob in the school corridor if she finds out you took me to the movies?"

With Coral being totally nuts, I knew that it was a possibility. But I couldn't let Carmella know that.

"No ... no!" I said. "Course not! She wouldn't do that. We're ... friends."

"So, when are you taking me to the movies?"

I think I flashed the biggest smile in the world since the Joker grinned at Batman in *The Dark Knight*. "Sat ... Saturday," I replied.

"Coolio," Carmella said.

For a short moment we just gazed into each other's eyes. It was interrupted by Mum. "Welton, hurry up and get showered and changed! I've got to put something on for dinner."

"OK, Mum," I replied, not taking my eyes off Carmella. "Car ... Carmella, you're on the same mobile number, right?"

"Yeah, why?"

"I've got a new phone. I'll text you later to tell you what films are on."

"Coolio."

I couldn't believe this was happening. Carmella McKenzie was saying coolio to me? It didn't seem real. I closed my eyes and opened them again. It was happening.

"Welton!" Mum barked. "Go and get your shower! I haven't got all night!"

"I'll text you later then," I said to Carmella. "After I have my dinner."

"I'll look out for it," she said.

I made my way to the changing room feeling as tall as the Monks Orchard Christmas tree in the town square. Someone should've lit beacons like they did in *Lord of the Rings*. Priests in long robes should've banged bells in churches and firework folk should've let off a shipload of sky sparklers.

I turned around and Carmella gave me a little wave. Parents were talking amongst themselves, but there was no sign of Dad. I wondered if he was all right. At least he hadn't made a scene. I was so happy he'd come to support me.

At the back of the hall stood a lone figure. It was Coral Chipglider. I hadn't seen her during the game. She had cut off her hair and was wearing purple make-up. Coral glared at me for two seconds before walking off. *Obi-Wan Kenobi, what should I do?* I prayed she wouldn't spit on Carmella.

CHAPTER 17

The Date

I showered twice that Saturday evening before I was satisfied I had deleted my BO. I brushed my molars three times. I even cleaned my tongue with my toothbrush. I used my deodorant stick on my armpits and all over my chest. I put on my black jeans and a pair of white trainers. I pulled on a plain black T-shirt. I was going to wear my lucky Darth Vader top, but I was worried Carmella would think I was a bit too old for it. I decided to wear my black denim jacket. I combed my hair and gazed into my bedroom mirror. Would Carmella want to sample this face?

The Brat collapsed in giggles as he sat on his new bed. "Who are you going to meet?" he asked.

"None of your business!" I replied.

"You're going to meet a girl!"

I had one last look in the mirror and stepped out into the hallway. I walked into the kitchen where Mum and Greyback sipped coffees.

"How much do you need, Welton?" Mum asked. "Ten pounds, is it?"

"Er, no, Mum. I need twenty."

"Twenty? Going to the pictures is not that expensive, is it?"

"Mum!" I said.

"I think Welton's taking someone out on a date," Greyback explained. "And, like most gentlemen, he wants to pay the way."

"Ahhhhh," said Mum. "That's so sweet. Who's the girl? Is it the one you were talking to after the game?"

"Mum! Can I have the money, please?"

"Do you want me to pick you up?"

"No," I told her.

"You sure?"

"I couldn't be surer, Mum. Stop mothering me."

"When the film finishes, you say your goodbyes and come straight home."

"Mum!"

"Angie," Greyback said to Mum. "Welton's a sensible boy. He won't hang around."

I think if I'd stayed any longer I would've hid Mum's Netflix remote control and chucked away all her hair extensions. *Can't she remember how traumatic it is to prepare for a first date?*

I headed out and made my way to the bus stop. It was 6.45 p.m. I was meeting Carmella at 7.30 p.m.

I had never waited so long for a bus. I started to think that Coral Chipglider was using the power of the Force to stop the bus arriving. Finally, it turned up at quarter past seven.

Getting off the bus, I checked the time on my mobile phone. *Oh no!* It was 7.31 p.m. I jet-footed to the shopping centre like I was being hunted by Bernice Cummings. I ran into people and nearly knocked a kid over. Some woman screamed at me, but I didn't care.

I reached the cinema at 7.35 p.m. I climbed the steps to the entrance. Frantically, I looked around. There was no sign of Carmella. I noticed some boys hanging out. I heard someone laughing behind me. I turned around. It was Corrington Wingburter. He was with Broxslater.

Oh no!

They were both drinking cans of soft drinks. Broxslater's thigh muscles bulged like the cheek of Godzilla who had been suffering from toothache.

"Look at Blakey!" cackled Wingburter. "He's all dressed up!"

Broxslater looked me up and down like he was deciding which part of me he wanted to munch first. "Going somewhere?" he asked.

I didn't answer. Broxslater's moustache twitched.

"Tax for the Chancellor, Blakey!" Broxslater demanded.

Inside my chest I could feel this fizzing ball of anger bouncing off my rib cage. It was getting bigger and bigger.

"Are you deaf?" Broxslater threatened me. "Don't make me repeat myself, Blakey. Tax for the Chancellor!"

Luke Skywalker magically appeared on my shoulder in his Jedi Knight cloak and whispered into my ear, *The time is now.*

"You're ... you're not getting anything from me, Broxslater!" I said, my voice high-pitched. I couldn't help but think of how neeky I sounded.

Out of the corner of my eye, I spotted Carmella approaching. Broxslater took a long step towards me. He clenched his fists. He took in a big mouthful of breath. "So you wanna be banged up on the steps of the cinema, do you, Blakey?" Broxslater asked.

Carmella moved closer. Something in my head told me that I just couldn't stand another humiliation. Not in front of Carmella. Not in front of anybody.

I tightened my right fist until the two thick veins in my wrist stuck out. Letting out a roar, I hit Broxslater with a right hook smack on the chin. He staggered back two paces and dropped on a step. He rubbed his chin with his right hand. "He hit me!"

I retreated two steps. My hand was killing me. I was sure I'd broken all the bones in it. Broxslater got up on his feet, rushed forward and dived on top of me, using my head as a punching ball. I tried to grab his arms to stop him. We both lost our balance and fell further down the steps.

"You hit me, Blakey!" Broxslater yelled. "You hit me!"

I think he couldn't believe I'd had the nerve to lick him. He made me pay for that. There wasn't a spot on my face that Broxslater didn't punch. My left eye was closing, but out of the corner of my right, I could see Carmella. Her hands were over her mouth. She yelled, "Leave him alone! Leave him alone!"

Corrington Wingburter held Carmella back. That was when I went nuts. I wriggled myself free and jumped to my feet. With all my might I swung with both fists. I didn't care where I hit Wingburter. I didn't stop. Wingburter ran off. I kept on punching. Broxslater dropped to the floor. Then I felt somebody's arms lifting me away. They were big limbs. For a short moment my feet didn't touch the ground.

I turned around and saw someone wearing a security guard's uniform. "Stop now, son," the man said. "He comes here quite regular, bullying kids. I think this evening he's learned his lesson."

Broxslater reeled away. He looked back at me and shook his head. He still couldn't believe what had happened to him.

When the security guard let go of me, I didn't realise how exhausted I was. I nearly fell to the ground again. My hands throbbed. My face felt like a thousand Olympic ice-skaters had slid across it. Then I felt a softer touch. Three fingers. A hand. Carmella's hand. She was touching my forehead. Her eyes looked enormous. I imagined diving into them. Carmella's lips were only a few centimetres away from mine. I could smell her perfume. She dabbed my bruises and cuts with a pocket tissue. She gave me a small smile.

"I think I should take you to the hospital," she said.

"No chance," I replied. "I've waited ages for this date."

"You sure you're all right?" Carmella asked.

"Is Yoda a Jedi Master? I've never felt better!"

Carmella helped me to my feet. We made it back up the steps to the cinema's box office. She kissed me on the cheek as we paid for our tickets. I had never felt so much pain, but it was all worth it. No more humiliations for Welton Blake. This was definitely gonna be the best night of my life.